THE GREAT
SHELBY HOLMES
AND THE HAUNTED HOUND

✦•THE GREAT•✦
SHELBY HOLMES
AND THE HAUNTED HOUND

ELIZABETH EULBERG

illustrated by ERWIN MADRID

BLOOMSBURY
CHILDREN'S BOOKS
NEW YORK LONDON OXFORD NEW DELHI SYDNEY

BLOOMSBURY CHILDREN'S BOOKS
Bloomsbury Publishing Inc., part of Bloomsbury Publishing Plc
1385 Broadway, New York, NY 10018

BLOOMSBURY, BLOOMSBURY CHILDREN'S BOOKS, and the Diana logo
are trademarks of Bloomsbury Publishing Plc

First published in the United States of America in September 2019
by Bloomsbury Children's Books

Bloomsbury books may be purchased for business or promotional use.
For information on bulk purchases please contact Macmillan Corporate and
Premium Sales Department at specialmarkets@macmillan.com

Library of Congress Cataloging-in-Publication Data
Names: Eulberg, Elizabeth, author.
Title: The great Shelby Holmes and the haunted hound / by Elizabeth Eulberg.
Description: New York : Bloomsbury, 2019.
Summary: Super sleuths Shelby Holmes and John Watson must survive
an overnight Halloween stakeout while investigating a local apartment building,
where residents hear an unearthly dog's howl at night.
Identifiers: LCCN 2019003806 (print) | LCCN 2019006415 (e-book)
ISBN 978-1-5476-0147-9 (hardcover) • ISBN 978-1-5476-0148-6 (e-book)
Subjects: | CYAC: Mystery and detective stories. | Haunted places—Fiction. | Friendship—
Fiction. | Harlem (New York, N.Y.)—Fiction.
Classification: LCC PZ7.E8685 Gsh 2019 (print) | LCC PZ7.E8685 (e-book) | DDC
[Fic]—dc23
LC record available at https://lccn.loc.gov/2019003806

Book design by Jeanette Levy
Typeset by Westchester Publishing Services
Printed and bound in the U.S.A. by Berryville Graphics Inc., Berryville, Virginia
2 4 6 8 10 9 7 5 3 1

To find out more about our authors and books
visit www.bloomsbury.com and sign up for our newsletters.

For all the librarians, especially my mother,
who have helped raise readers (and detectives)

CHAPTER
1

THERE WERE MANY THINGS I'D LEARNED ABOUT SHELBY Holmes in the time I'd known her. Besides that she was prickly and abrupt and short-tempered.

One: she was never late. Two: she liked her routines. Three: she never missed a day of school for anything, not even if she got sick.

Because of those three things, I found myself walking upstairs to Shelby's apartment on Monday morning. She always stopped by my place on her way to school, but so far nothing. And I didn't want to be late because of her.

I knocked on the door to 221B.

"Come in, Watson," Shelby called out.

When I opened the door, I was relieved to find Shelby dressed and ready for school. Although she was frozen in an armchair in the living room next to the fireplace. She sat face-to-face with her nemesis. Well, one of them.

She had a lot of adversaries, because of, well, the exact qualities I listed above.

But perhaps her biggest foe stared right back at her.

Her brother, Michael.

Yep. It was a sibling standoff.

Neither of them made a sound. It was so quiet you could hear the cars driving all the way over on Lenox. I began playing with the strap of my backpack. Honestly, being around the two of them generally unsettled me. But this was another level. They glared intensely at each other. Eyes were slit and everything.

What now? Usually they were at odds over some random science fact. Or having to live in the same space.

"Um, Shelby," I began, but Shelby held her hand up to silence me.

She then jumped up.

"Aha!" she exclaimed. "Well done, Watson!"

Well done? What did I do? Not like I wasn't going to take a compliment from her, since they were pretty rare.

"Your interruption gave me the exact clue I required," Shelby said. "Granted, stronger minds wouldn't be so easily distracted. Yet I'm dealing with a lesser opponent."

Okaaaaay.

Shelby walked over to the giant bookshelf near the door. She ran a finger over the books. "Yes, yes . . . ," she said while Michael shifted in his seat.

She faced her brother with a grin as she pulled a large red leather book off the shelf. She opened it and flipped through the pages.

"Hello, what's this?" she remarked before pulling out a tiny piece of paper, about the size of a thumbnail.

Michael folded his arms. "Lucky break," he replied in his monotone voice.

"Ah, see, dear brother, luck has nothing to do with it. But it is quite easy if you know what to look for. Right, Watson?"

"Yeah," I replied. I wanted to get moving so we wouldn't

be late for school. Although Shelby was correct. Working on cases with her has taught me not to simply see but to observe. Whatever she found had to do with deductive reasoning.

Shelby turned her back to me and explained to a not-amused Michael, "When Watson spoke, it distracted you enough to glance at the bookshelf. That led me to deduce you hid the note there. Thanks to our parents assigning you to clean the living room this weekend, the dusting was subpar. A quick examination of the bookshelf showed which book had been removed recently." She dragged her finger along the bookshelf and showed us her dirty finger.

Michael yawned in response. I glanced at my watch.

"We have ample time to get to school, Watson," Shelby stated.

How did she—*?* Shelby wasn't even facing me. I swear she has eyes in the back of her head.

"The glass on the picture above the fireplace," Shelby said, looking over her shoulder.

"What?"

"I could see your reflection in the glass. That was how I knew you were getting antsy."

Unbelievable. Although it wasn't really. It was just Shelby Holmes.

She grabbed her oversized purple backpack. "Okay,

Watson. We're quickly arriving at the minimum time we should allot for walking to school."

Ah, *duh*. That's why I was up there in the first place.

Shelby continued, "Be advised that I have a treat for you this afternoon when we get back home. I'm going to teach you how to examine knife wounds on a carcass to determine the height of an assailant."

I stopped dead in my tracks. "What?"

"Oh relax. My parents bought a pot roast for dinner. I'm going to use that."

Shelby and I really, *really* needed to talk about what I would consider a treat. Because it would never have to do with a carcass. *Gross.* Besides, we would never work with a stab victim. (At least I hoped. Oh, how I hoped.)

Michael yawned again as he brushed a hand against his light blond, nearly white hair. "You're still pretending to be a detective? How charming."

Charming?

What Shelby and I did was anything but cutesy. We dealt with real cases. Since I'd begun working with Shelby, we'd caught a dognapper, helped out a teacher, vanquished a nemesis worthy of Shelby's talents, and saved a figure skater from injury.

So yeah. We'd become kind of a big deal. At least around our Harlem neighborhood.

But Shelby just gave Michael one last glare before we walked out of the apartment.

"So what was that all about?" I asked.

"What was what?" She reached into her jacket pocket and pulled out a candy bar—what Shelby Holmes called a balanced breakfast. "Please be more specific as it's all in the details, Watson."

"You and Michael. The stare down. The note. What did it say?"

"The piece of paper didn't say anything," she replied.

"But then why were you looking for it?"

"We were playing a game."

"A game?" Yeah, siblings played games and stuff, but Shelby and Michael weren't the fun-game types. Or the type to do anything that normal siblings would do.

There had to be a catch.

Shelby furrowed her brows. "You must've heard of hide-and-seek."

Ah, yeah. Who hadn't?

Wait a second. "You play hide-and-seek with a tiny piece of paper?"

Shelby snorted. "Indeed. How do *you* play it?"

"Um, like everybody else."

Shelby scrunched up her face. Clearly she didn't realize how the game was usually played.

Of course she didn't.

Shelby Holmes was many things, but a regular kid was not one of them.

"Yeah, so a person or a group of people hide while someone tries to find them," I stated.

She tilted her head. "So your version of the game is for *people* to hide? That doesn't seem like a challenge at all. In fact, it appears to be quite pedestrian."

"It's not my version. It's how it's played!"

I mean, *really!*

I tried to hide my annoyance as we arrived at the Harlem Academy of the Arts with only a couple minutes to spare. As soon as we entered the hallway, Shelby gave a little grunt.

"What is it?"

She pointed her finger at my friend John Bryant, who was walking down the hallway with his head down.

"It appears your acquaintance had a rough evening."

Bryant's shaggy blond bangs covered his face, so I couldn't get a good look at him. He did seem to be dragging his feet a bit, but I knew Bryant better than Shelby, and he didn't seem all that different to me.

Although the most important thing I've learned about Shelby was this: never argue with her. She was always right.

And yes, it was as annoying as you could imagine.

"How do you know that?" I asked, because it was the only way I'd learn.

"From observing, Watson." She paused. "But I guess you can do the uninspired thing and simply inquire of him directly."

She shook her head in disappointment as she walked to her locker.

Typical Shelby.

CHAPTER 2

YOU KNOW THAT THING I SAID ABOUT SHELBY ALWAYS BEING right?

Yeah, well . . . there *was* something wrong with Bryant. When I sat down next to him at lunch, he had no color in his already pale face. His light blue eyes were puffy and darting all over the cafeteria.

"Hey, man," I said. "How was your weekend?"

"Yeah. I didn't get a lot of sleep." His attention settled on his lunch bag, even though he made no effort to take any food out.

"That's the worst," I said, patting his shoulder. "I hardly slept during our figure skating case last week. It took me an entire weekend of sleeping like ten hours a day to start feeling normal again."

Even thinking about my alarm clock blasting at five in the morning caused me to yawn. Not to sound like my mom, but sleep was important.

9

And by the look on Bryant's face, he really needed a good night's sleep.

"What's up?" Carlos said, dropping his lunch and sketchbook on the table with a thud.

Bryant jumped at the noise.

"Calm down, dude." Carlos held out his hands in surrender. "What? Did you watch some scary movie last night?"

Bryant shook his head as his entire posture drooped down even farther.

"Speaking of," Jason began as he sat down, "we've got to talk strategy for Halloween."

Carlos patted his stomach. "I can't wait to get my just rewards for an awesome costume. I'm obviously talking about candy, candy, and yep, more candy."

I looked over at Shelby, who ate alone at her usual table. She had only come over to join us for lunch once, despite an open invitation. She was on friendly enough terms with some of the guys (which was saying a lot for her). But Shelby always replied that spending lunch "surrounded by incessant chatter" would disrupt her "precious research time."

That girl never stopped studying.

Halloween had to be Shelby's favorite holiday since it was focused on her favorite thing: sugar. Since her parents still had her on a sugar ban (even though she had found ways to get around it and was possibly eating more sugar now), I doubted they would let her go out this Thursday. Not like they could control her that much.

"What do you think, Watson?" Jason asked me as he tucked one of his locs behind his ear.

I shrugged. I hadn't really thought much about it. I always like getting dressed up with my buddies, but with my diabetes, I couldn't really eat a lot of candy. Mom would let me have a couple mini-bars during the week, but I would end up handing out my stash to my friends. I guess I could give it all to Shelby, especially when I needed her to be in a better mood, which was pretty much all the time.

"Oh!" Carlos exclaimed. "Maybe you can wear that costume Shelby made you for your last case and go as a figure skater. HA!"

"I am *not* going as a figure skater," I stated. I was never going to wear that sparkly, sequined monstrosity. *Never.* "Next idea, one that won't cause me to have nightmares."

Jason let out his loud, infectious laugh, which caused Bryant to bristle. Seriously, what was going on with him? Unless he didn't want me to even mention my cases. He was not Shelby's biggest fan, but still. It's what I did.

"John!" Carlos said to John Wu, who had just arrived. "What are we doing for Halloween? We should do something as a group!"

John pushed up his wire-rimmed glasses. "I've decided to use this Halloween as a way to fully encompass one of the greatest parts for an actor: Hamlet." He dramatically held out his arm. " 'To be, or not to be, that is the question . . .' "

Carlos hit his forehead with his palm. "*No*, the question is what are we going as for Halloween?" He sighed. "Actors."

"We could go as a team," Jason offered. "Knicks? Giants? Yankees?"

"Boring!" Carlos countered. He opened up his sketchbook and started drawing with one hand while the other held his sandwich.

Jason leaned back in his chair. "Hey, I'm trying to think of things that don't require a lot of work. I'm slammed by homework. Unlike Watson over here, I have to come up with my inspirations for writing class."

Yeah, I was lucky that I had Shelby and our adventures to keep my writing journal full.

All eyes settled on me. Okay, Halloween . . .

"Zombies," I threw out.

"Oh, I like it!" Carlos slammed his hand on the table.

Bryant looked like he was going to be sick. He hadn't touched his lunch. Maybe he had food poisoning or the flu and that had kept him up all night.

"Or ghosts!" Jason added.

With that, Bryant put his head in his hands and leaned on the table.

"Bryant?" I asked.

The rest of us looked at each other, trying to figure out what was going on with him.

Bryant finally glanced up at us. His face was about as white as a ghost's.

"Do you believe in them?" he asked in a soft voice.

"Believe in what?" John Wu replied.

We all leaned in to hear him.

"Ghosts," he finally said. "Do you believe in ghosts?"

Was he being serious?

After a few beats of silence, Carlos let out a snort. "Totally. And zombies." He then took a big bite of his sandwich. "Braaaaaiiiins!"

Everybody laughed, except for Bryant. He got up and started walking out of the cafeteria without a word.

"What's up with him?" Jason asked.

"*He's* the one acting like a zombie," Carlos replied.

Even if Shelby hadn't said anything, I would've known something wasn't right. "I'm going to check on him."

I grabbed the rest of my lunch and headed out to get to the bottom of this.

"Hey, Bryant! Hold up!" I called after him. I slung my arm around his shoulder as we walked down the hallway. "What's going on? Can I help with something?"

Bryant started nodding. "Yeah. You're probably the only person who could. Can you spend the night tonight?"

"Tonight? It's a school night."

"It can't wait for the weekend. Please."

"I don't think my mom—" But I stopped myself when I saw how desperate Bryant appeared. He needed a friend, and I was going to be that friend for him. He and I had a bit of a rocky patch when the rest of the guys helped Shelby and me out with a case. So I owed him this. "Sure, yeah."

Bryant finally looked at me. "Thanks. I really need your help."

"Okay. Like with homework?" Bryant was pretty smart. I wasn't sure how much I could help him.

"No." He paused and looked around the hallway. "It's—I don't really know what it is. But you're a detective so I just thought, you know, you could maybe figure out something."

"I could come after school?" I offered.

He shook his head. "No, it has to be at night."

"Well, let me talk to Shelby—"

"No!" Bryant protested. "I don't want her involved. *At all.*"

That wasn't a shock. Bryant didn't get along with Shelby. Yeah, not many people got along with Shelby, but Bryant *really* didn't like her. She was his main competition in violin at school, and as you can imagine, Shelby wasn't very gracious to those below her. Or basically anybody.

"What kind of case? Did you lose something?"

"You need to be there."

Ah, so that wasn't helpful at all. But I guess I'll get some answers tonight.

"Sure. Whatever you need."

Bryant looked off into the distance.

"You cool, man?" I asked.

He leaned in. "Do you believe in ghosts?"

This again?

"Not really," I replied. I mean, Dad and I always watched

scary movies together and all that, but I didn't believe ghosts and zombies were real. That didn't mean I couldn't dress up as one. And to be honest, I didn't really believe in most of the New York sports teams right now. They'd had some tough losses recently.

Bryant nodded. "Yeah, that's what I thought before . . ."

He didn't finish. He simply turned around and walked away from me.

A chill ran down my spine. It hit me, Bryant looked exactly like he had seen something truly terrifying. Something that had to be seen with his own eyes to be believed.

Something like a ghost.

⌐·CHAPTER·⌐
3

"DO YOU BELIEVE IN GHOSTS?"

I'd repeated this question in my head all day. Even though I didn't believe. Nope. Ghosts weren't real.

Right?

Now I posed the question to Shelby on our walk home after school.

She didn't break her stride. "I unequivocally do not."

"Yeah, but how do you know? For sure."

"There is absolutely no scientific proof of the existence of ghosts. Period," Shelby said with a nod of her head, like she was done discussing the topic.

We were not.

"But there are people who claim they've seen ghosts," I argued. Isn't that what ghosts were? The unknown. People alleged they'd seen them. There had been reports of the unexplained, and all those shows on TV about people hunting ghosts. How could they hunt something that wasn't real?

"The power of suggestion," Shelby stated with an impatient huff. "You tell someone they're walking into a haunted house, they're ready to start believing they are seeing or hearing things that don't exist. Then there are people who have recently lost a loved one. Those individuals are seeking comfort, and believing that their spouse or parent or whoever is close by may make them feel better."

While I agreed with her in theory, part of me had been on edge after talking with Bryant. He'd experienced *something* that freaked him out.

I was probably letting my imagination get away with me. That horror movie marathon this past weekend was a bad idea. But Dad and I had a tradition of video chatting while watching some pretty bad horror movies. There was one that took place in an abandoned apartment building that kind of scared me. I wanted to turn my bedroom light on, but didn't want Dad to think I'd gone soft. I'd moved the screen so he couldn't see me cover my ears a few times. It wasn't the gore that would cause me to jump the most, it was always when there'd be a loud sound out of nowhere.

Yeah, so all the horror movies had me on edge. That and all the ghost decorations around the neighborhood for Halloween.

"Are you trying to explain your friend's behavior away on a ghost?" Shelby asked.

"No," I lied.

She groaned as she threw her head back. "Oh, come on, Watson. You know me better than to make an attempt to deceive me."

Busted.

She continued, "Your friend has clearly not slept well in a few days. He's jittery. You followed him out after he left in the middle of lunch, and now you're asking me about ghosts. You don't have to be an intellect of my caliber to connect those dots."

"Okay, okay," I said. "Yeah, he asked me if I believed in ghosts right after I agreed to spend the night tonight." An unexpected chill ran down my spine thinking about it.

"You have nothing to worry about," Shelby stated confidently. "There are absolutely no such things as ghosts, goblins, zombies, vampires, fairies, the Loch Ness Monster, or whatever other creatures have been created to sell books and movies. I am currently unable to cite specific statistics, as I will not let such silly fantasies of the imagination take up precious space in my brain attic."

Ah, yes. Shelby's brain attic. It's filled with the most random facts one can imagine about science, geography, rock formations—you name it, she had studied it and put the information in there. There were certain things she didn't find "worthy," like anything about sports, friends, being normal, and now ghosts.

But it was Shelby so she was (say it with me!) right.

Although didn't she eventually have to be wrong? At least once? Nobody was perfect, not even the great Shelby Holmes.

Oh please don't have the first time she's wrong be about this.

If so, it was going to be a long night.

"So what's this school project you have?" Mom asked when she got home from work at the hospital.

"Oh, it's, ah . . ."

Okay, Watson. You probably should've figured she was going to ask this question. Every good detective has to think a few steps ahead. Obviously Mom was going to be interested in why I had to spend a school night at Bryant's.

"Yeah, it's . . . a science experiment for Mr. Crosby's class. We have to do all these charts about the growth of a . . . potato. So we thought we could get ahead if I spent the night. The potatoes are at his house."

A wave of guilt overcame me. I'd promised Mom I wouldn't lie to her anymore. When I first started working with Shelby on her cases, I kinda, sorta hadn't told her. Then she found out the truth while I was in an ambulance (long story), and I'd been honest with her ever since. But how would I explain why I was going over to Bryant's when *I* had no idea what was going on?

This was simply me being a good friend to Bryant. While we don't share our opinions on Shelby, he was a close friend who was also an only child living with his divorced mom. Our other friends had big families. Carlos lived with his parents, three siblings, and grandmother. John Wu lived with his two dads and sister while Jason lived with his parents, two sisters, his auntie, and cousin.

At least Bryant's dad lived nearby in Brooklyn, while mine was in Kentucky at the army post I used to call home. Still, sometimes you needed a friend.

Mom put her hand to my forehead. "Well, okay, but I want to check your glucose levels before you leave. And call me tonight before your bedtime insulin shot so I can monitor your levels."

"You know, if I had the insulin pump . . . ," I threw out there. Checking my glucose levels and doing my daily insulin shots have become standard for me, but every once in a while I got jealous when a kid with diabetes had the insulin pump. It did all the monitoring for you. But Mom trusted herself more than technology, especially when it came to my health.

Mom shook her head. She picked up her phone and typed for a bit. "Let's not make school night sleepovers a habit. Next time, you can have Bryant over or anybody else if you have a project."

Her phone chirped. She looked at it and smiled.

"Who's that?" I asked.

She smiled bigger while she typed a response. "Just a friend, sweetie."

Uh-huh. I studied Mom. Was she blushing? She tucked a strand of hair behind her ear.

"What friend?" I pressed. Because Mom wasn't acting like she was texting with just a friend.

Hmm, maybe Bryant's paranoia was contagious?

Mom laughed. "A friend from work. Shouldn't you pack your bag and head to Bryant's? Do you want me to walk you over?"

"It's okay." I didn't move. "So what are you going to do tonight?"

"Nothing." She glanced to her right. "Probably watch a movie."

Wait a second. Why was Mom lying to me? The glance to the right. The avoidance of eye contact. She was keeping something from me.

My mind began to swirl with possibilities. There was one more plausible than the rest, but I wasn't prepared to deal with that.

Because if my suspicions were correct, Mom having a boyfriend would be much more frightening than a ghost.

CHAPTER 4

MY LEAST FAVORITE PART OF LATE FALL AND WINTER WAS how much earlier the sun would go down. It wasn't even seven o'clock and it'd been dark for over an hour.

I didn't like it.

Okay, I was clearly letting Bryant's behavior get to me. It was dark. So what? It was nighttime. That was what happened at night, the sun went down.

Get a grip, Watson.

I walked the several blocks up Lenox Avenue to Bryant's apartment building. When I turned on 141st Street, I noticed the block was quiet. Almost too quiet. Most of the buildings had their windows boarded up. I'd only been over to his apartment a few times, but now, I noticed Sold signs on the buildings that hadn't been there before.

Bryant lived in a gray stone four-story apartment building. It was one of those old buildings that had the name engraved at the front entrance: Baskerville Estates.

I took a deep breath to erase my nerves as I rang the bell

for apartment 3. I was buzzed in and walked up the stairs to find Bryant standing outside his apartment, holding the door open.

As I stepped inside, Bryant gave me a weary smile. "Hey, man."

His mom rushed over to give me a hug. "Oh, John! Thanks so much for coming!"

"You're welcome. Mrs.—Ms.—" I fumbled, remembering that Bryant's mom used her maiden name, which I couldn't remember.

"You can call me Claire."

"Yes, ma'am," I replied since Mom insisted I refer to adults by Ms. or Mr. It was a sign of respect. Mom would be the first person to call me out if I wasn't being respectful, especially with my elders. And since I was only eleven, pretty much everybody was my elder.

Except Shelby, who was only nine. Not like she would ever show anybody respect, no matter their age.

Present company—aka me—included.

Bryant and his mom looked very similar, and not solely because they both were clearly exhausted. She had his pale complexion and same blond hair, with hers up in a tight ponytail. They both wore matching necklaces I'd never seen before—a black rectangular stone with a pointed tip on a silver strand.

"Is that new?" I asked.

"Ah, yeah," Bryant said as he looked down.

"It's black tourmaline," his mom replied as she picked hers up from her chest and studied it. "It's a stone that's supposed to help ward off negative energies. It may sound silly, but we'll do whatever may help."

I could only nod along since I didn't know what the negative energy was . . . and I wasn't that excited to find out.

"Well, please make yourself welcome," Bryant's mom said as she walked over to the living room, which connected to the kitchen. It was a lot like our place. Most New York City apartments were open like that. I think it made the space feel bigger since three rooms were crammed into one area.

I sent Mom a quick text that I'd arrived at Bryant's and hoped she had a good night. When I left, she was still dressed in the clothes she wore to work. Usually after dinner, she'd put on sweats.

Yet another reason to be suspicious she wasn't just spending the night in by herself.

But first things first.

I decided to treat Bryant like one of our suspects. Start out with small questions. Get him relaxed, and he'd start talking so I could figure out exactly why I was here. And hopefully it had nothing to do with a ghost.

"So what's the negative energy?" I asked.

"There's been some weird stuff happening in the building.

And well, I thought you could help us out with some of the things you've learned from Shelby." He scowled when he said her name. "There has to be a reasonable explanation of all that's going on."

"Okay." I gulped. I hadn't really had a case on my own. And I wasn't even sure where to begin. So I guess we start with the most basic questions. "What's been happening?"

Bryant's mom came over and put her arm around her son. "It started this weekend. Weird noises. It's an old building so we've gotten used to creaking and hearing our neighbors, but this was different. Stomping footsteps. The lights blinking on and off. Unexplained sounds, like from some kind of animal. A howling."

"Could it be from a dog?" I asked. Even I sometimes heard Shelby's English bulldog, Sir Arthur, barking upstairs if he was in a disagreement with Shelby about something. He was the only living creature who Shelby would give in to.

Bryant and his mom exchanged a look. "Not exactly."

"A wolf?" Were there any wolves in New York City?

"It didn't sound like a wolf," Bryant said in a quiet voice. "It was like a giant beast. You kind of have to hear it to understand."

"Yes," his mom agreed. "And well, there's just this feeling I have. This heaviness in my chest. It's like someone is watching us."

"Yeah, me too," Bryant admitted. "It's weird. I don't feel right."

I nodded. Maybe it was the power of suggestion like Shelby said, but I felt a little light-headed. I wondered if they had an extra necklace for me.

"Can you tell where the sounds are coming from?" I inquired. I couldn't make deductions based on how someone felt, but if we could pinpoint where it was happening, we'd know what was making the noise. It could simply be something crawling in the wall like mice or, I don't know, a squirrel or something.

Gross.

"Yes." Bryant's mom gestured for us to sit down on their couch. "Would you like something to eat or drink? I have sugar-free cookies."

"I'm okay for now, thanks." I sat down and got out my notebook. I usually used it to keep notes after spending the day with Shelby so I could properly report in my online journal, but this time Shelby wasn't with me. I didn't want to miss anything. Also, I hated to admit that I might need to call her if I got stuck.

Which Bryant wouldn't be okay with and Shelby would just loooooove. So yeah, I had to do this on my own.

"After I felt agitated all day Saturday, the power started to flicker," Bryant's mom explained. "I didn't think anything of it. It happens sometimes, especially in an old building. Then the power went out completely. We started hearing footsteps above us. But not normal footsteps. I'd know, I've lived in apartment buildings my entire life. It was purposeful, slow steps. Almost foreboding. Then a tapping noise started."

I looked at the ceiling above. It took me a while to get used to hearing the Holmeses walking around. Even though they have rugs and usually take off their shoes when they get home, every once in a while you'd hear someone walking around. It was part of living in an apartment building.

"Who lives upstairs?" That had to be the most obvious explanation.

Bryant and his mom exchanged a look. "That's the thing: nobody," Bryant's mom stated. "There's a new tenant arriving in a few weeks, but for now it's vacant. Our landlord even checked upstairs while it was happening, and the apartment was empty."

Okay, that was freaky. How could there be footsteps and tapping above if nobody was up there?

"Did anybody else hear it?"

She shook her head. "Not the tapping or footsteps, but everybody heard the howling. It's kind of hard to ignore. Our across-the-hall neighbor, Mr. Mortimer, is elderly and a bit hard of hearing, but even he could hear it. We talked to the rest of the tenants. The Lyonses, they live next to apartment 5, also heard the tapping, but not the footsteps. The guy who lives on the top floor only heard the beast."

I searched my brain for what could be causing noise in an empty apartment, but I had nothing.

Zip. Zilch. Nada. Diddly-squat.

"Would you like a sweatshirt?" Bryant's mom asked. I realized I had wrapped my arms around myself. It was cold in here. Both Bryant and his mom were wearing sweaters. She even had on a pair of fingerless gloves.

"Sorry, man," Bryant said. "I should've warned you that it's a little cool. The heat's working, it's just . . ."

Another thing that didn't make sense.

Uneasy feelings. Chills in a heated apartment. Sounds from an empty unit.

Come on, think, Watson. What would cause all of this?

"There's something else," Bryant said as both he and his mom shuddered. Whatever it was, it couldn't have been good. "We found out that the original owner of this building died in that apartment decades ago. And he had a dog."

Gulp.

At that exact moment, the power flickered off. The room became pitch black, save for a hint of light streaming in from the streetlights outside.

"Stay there," Bryant's mom said. "I'll get the candles and flashlight."

I will not panic. I will not panic, I kept reminding myself. *There are no such things as ghosts. There's a reasonable explanation for everything.*

STOMP.

Whoooosh.

STOMP.

Whoooosh.

STOMP.

Whoooosh.

Footsteps. Slow. Deliberate. It sounded like a foot was being dragged. So yeah. Not at all normal.

Bryant's mom lit a few candles. The lights flickered on their worried faces. I didn't want to think what I must've looked like.

Scratch, scratch . . .

What was that? It was soft at first, but then louder.

SCRATCH.

SCRATCH.

SCRATCH.

Like an animal was trying to get in. A very hungry animal.

"We hadn't heard that before," Bryant said in a near whisper. His mom had her arm around him.

Then . . .

Grrrrrrrrr . . .

Grrrrrrrrr . . .

HOOOOWWWWLLLL!

The growl turned into an ear-piercing howl. My pulse quickened. Bryant's mom was right: no dog sounded like that. The creature seemed almost annoyed. Hungry.

I had no clue what to think. But I didn't want to meet the beast that could make such a horrifying sound.

Right then, the big candle on the kitchen table blew out, plunging us all into darkness again. The noise above increased, and I put my hands over my ears. My heart was practically jumping out of my chest. All I wanted in that moment was for it to stop and to get as far away from this haunted apartment as quickly as possible.

Grrrrrrrr . . .

Grrrrrrrrr . . .

HOOOWWWLLL!

I was close to letting out a scream, and then Bryant turned on his flashlight.

Our eyes locked. We were both terrified.

He was right.

There was a ghost in his apartment building!

BANG! BANG! BANG!

I yelped as the banging was coming from the front door. Bryant and his mom must've been super relieved to have me here.

A man's voice on the other side of the door asked, "Everybody okay in there?"

"Our landlord, Jay Barrymore," Bryant's mom replied as she got up and opened the door.

The noise from above continued.

STOMP.

Whoooosh.

STOMP.

Whoooosh.

STOMP.

Whoooosh.

A young guy with a super-cool fade haircut shone his flashlight around the apartment. "Okay, good. You're safe. I'm going to check upstairs. I'm so sorry, I wish I could figure out what was going on."

The door across the hall opened up. An elderly man with a white beard held up his own flashlight. "What's going on? Who has a dog?"

"I'm looking into it, Mr. Mortimer," Mr. Barrymore said, but he didn't look confident. Or happy that he had to climb the stairs to go to where the noise was coming from. I didn't blame him.

SCRATCH.

SCRATCH.

SCRATCH.

I should've gone upstairs with him to see if I could figure out what was happening, but imagining what might be up there—a four-headed beast with drool coming off his sharp

fangs, or a ghost wanting to exact revenge, maybe both!—
I was frozen on the couch in fear. Some solo detective I
turned out to be.

After a few minutes, Barrymore returned. He scratched
his head. "I don't understand it. There's nobody there. It's
empty."

STOMP.

Whoooosh.

STOMP.
Whoooosh.
STOMP.
Whoooosh.

How was that coming from an abandoned unit?

The lights flashed on and off for a few seconds as the
howling intensified.

HOOWWWLLL!
HOOOWWWLLL!

We all tensed at the sound. Then the lights went back on
and the building fell quiet.

Too quiet.

I should've been relieved, but I wasn't. I didn't have any
answers, and I was absolutely, 100 percent freaked out.

Well, the impossible had happened. Shelby Holmes was
wrong.

As much as I couldn't wait to rub it in her face, I had one major, scary problem.

I was trapped in a building by a creature that couldn't possibly be from this world.

⌐CHAPTER⌐
5

SLEEP THAT NIGHT WAS PRETTY MUCH IMPOSSIBLE.

Even after the noises from above stopped, every creak in the floor or muffled sound from a TV jolted me wide awake. I also felt this heaviness and paranoia that was hard to explain. At one point a police car drove down the street and the siren practically made my heart leap out of my chest.

"You okay, man?" I asked Bryant as we headed to school. I felt guilty I didn't have any answers for him. "Last night was intense."

He gave a small nod. "I feel better knowing that it's not just in our heads."

"So, I got to be honest, I'm a little stumped," I admitted. "I know you have issues with Shelby, but—"

"No!" he protested. "There's no way I want her involved."

"Okay, but I'm stuck. Can I just talk to her about it? Get her thoughts? Maybe she has some ideas. As you're more than aware, she thinks she knows everything."

Bryant let out a little snort. "No kidding." He paused for a bit. "She'd make fun of me, and I'd never hear the end of it."

"Listen, I only want to bounce ideas off her. I promise you I'll keep her in check and she won't make fun of you."

He tilted his head back and forth, and finally sighed. "I guess. As long as she doesn't give me any grief."

"Deal."

Did I just promise Bryant that Shelby would behave and show some restraint?

Yikes.

"Stop it!" I pleaded.

I really should've seen this coming.

I clenched my jaw. "Can you please stop? I'm being serious."

Shelby continued to laugh in response to my detailed description of last night, which was exactly why Bryant didn't want to get her involved.

Point goes to Bryant.

"But, Shelby, someone had died in the building, in the very unit where the noise is happening. And he had a dog!"

I mean, come on! That alone made this super creepy.

"Who was the person?" she asked.

I stared back at her in reply.

Shelby continued, "And when was this alleged death? The cause? What facts have backed up this claim, or is it simply hearsay?"

"I don't know!" I snapped. "Why would someone lie about that?"

"People lie about things all the time," Shelby stated. "I'm disappointed that you haven't checked your sources, Watson."

"Okay, I'll check up on the facts, but if it's true?"

Shelby snorted. "Watson, people die in homes all the time. Why, I once inquired into the history of 221 Baker Street—"

"STOP!" I held up my hand. "Do *not* tell me about any deaths in our building. I do *not* want to know!"

"Knowledge is power," Shelby said with a shrug. "I prefer to live in reality."

I had zero patience for her dismissive behavior because I was exhausted. "Do you really think I'd make this up?"

"No, you clearly *believe* there's some human and/or dog ghost lurking in Bryant's apartment building." Shelby gestured at me. "Your physical posturing indicates you accept you're telling the truth. But as I explained yesterday, there is no such thing as ghosts. There's a logical explanation for everything."

"That's what I thought, too." I did, I really did. Until I heard it. And *felt* it. "But I couldn't come up with a why or how any of that was happening."

"Oh well, if *you* couldn't," Shelby said with a roll of her eyes.

"Give me some credit, Shelby!" I snapped. "And oh, I don't know, maybe you could for once acknowledge how much better I've gotten. Or do you need me to give you a list of all the clues I've figured out before you."

Okay, yeah, the score of us making deductions was still like a bazillion to five in Shelby's favor, but still. I knew things. Noise and footsteps coming from an empty apartment *where someone had died*? Chills with the heat on? A really bad feeling? How could *anybody* explain that?

I continued, "You can also deduce from my appearance that I've had a rough night. So it would be helpful if you could just be nice to me for a change. Or should we have the talk about bullies again?"

Shelby's smug face fell. Maybe I was being a little harsh.

No. Even on my worst day, I was still a better listener and friend than Shelby.

"All right, Watson," Shelby said. She reached out her hand and awkwardly patted me on the back. "Yes, you've had an uncomfortable evening. You believe that there's something otherworldly going on. If you couldn't make any deductions after spending the evening, I must assume that whoever is responsible for this is quite skilled."

The fact that Shelby was listening to me and even gave me a rare compliment made me feel just a little bit better. Although anything was better than her taunts.

"Watson, let me inquire: Now that you're not in the apartment is that heavy feeling you described gone?"

"Yeah." It took a few blocks of fresh air, but the farther away from Baskerville Estates I got, the less agitated I felt. I was still tired, but that was understandable.

Shelby looked thoughtful for a moment. Like she was really going to help me with this. "One reasonable explanation could be someone using infrasound to elicit these responses from you."

"Using what?"

"Infrasound. It's a sound that falls below the audible twenty hertz frequency. There are theories it can cause physiological discomfort."

I stared blankly back at Shelby.

"Ah, could you explain?"

She perked up. "I'd be more than delighted! Most humans have a hearing range from approximately twenty hertz to approximately twenty thousand hertz, or waves per second. Anything below that is considered infrasound. It doesn't register to us as a sound, but our bodies register it unconsciously. People who experience it can have feelings of panic, changes in heart rate, even chills down one's spine. One noted astrophysicist has stated people can even have visual hallucinations at eighteen point nine-eight hertz."

Um, okaaaaay. Seriously. How did she know this stuff?

Although this would at least explain the feeling.

"What causes these, ah, sounds?"

"Many things, like severe weather and humpback whales, but it can be replicated with engines and fans. You can buy infrasound generators on the internet."

So that was it? A machine? It seemed too easy.

"But you're missing the most important question," Shelby stated.

"What was that?"

"If this indeed is due to infrasound, why would someone be doing this to the residents of Bryant's building?"

Of course! One of the most important questions in trying to solve a mystery was the *why*, because that often would lead to the *who*. Who would be doing this?

"Is that why we heard the footsteps, clawing, and growling from an empty apartment and why we thought the lights went off?" No way could some low sound waves do that. I will never forget the howling of that . . . beast.

Shelby shook her head. "No. *That* I need to think on."

Wait. What? Was I still asleep? Was this a dream?

Shelby didn't have an immediate answer for something.

Well, I was certainly awake now.

~·CHAPTER·~
6

POOR BRYANT.

He had three sleepless nights with whatever was going on in his apartment. I only had one, and I could barely get through my morning classes, despite the shock of Shelby's confession. At least tonight I'd get to sleep in the comfort of my own home with hopefully no nightmares.

Dad and I would have to skip watching another so-bad-it's-good horror movie tonight.

Oh no. I was going to have to tell Mom about this, wasn't I? There was only so much I could get away with, and the fact that I'd probably be jumpy for a few days was going to be slightly suspicious.

But wait. Shelby had a logical answer for the weird feeling we had in the apartment. Although I didn't see any fans. And how could everybody else in the building feel it?

And the creature? And the footsteps . . . And! And! And! Ugh.

I dragged my feet to our lunch table. Carlos, Jason, and John Wu were already in the thick of some discussion. I sat down and started unpacking my lunch. Bryant wasn't that far behind and sat next to me. He and I picked at our food in silence, while the rest of the guys talked about classes and homework and things I wished I could think about.

But nope. Even with that infrasound information, it still didn't sit well with me.

"Okay, so zombies for Halloween?" Carlos said loudly, not noticing that Bryant and I recoiled at the mention of zombies.

"Zombies are played out," Jason replied. "We need to be creative."

Bryant looked like he was going to be sick. I hadn't had a chance to tell him about Shelby's theory, but I doubted it was going to give him much comfort. There were still a lot of unanswered questions.

"Um, guys, can we talk about something else?" I suggested.

Carlos looked between Bryant and me. "What's going on with you two? Have you seen a zombie?"

The rest of the guys laughed. I leaned over to Bryant and said, "Maybe we should just tell them?" Then they would know better than to tease us.

"They wouldn't believe me," Bryant said in a quiet voice.

"That's not true."

Bryant gave me a look because I didn't truly believe him until I experienced it myself.

Before I had a chance to respond our entire lunch table began to rattle. I could see the hands of all five of us on the table. The shaking intensified. Bryant froze next to me.

"What's going on?" Carlos asked. "Ooooh, haunted!"

Tap, tap, tap . . .

Tap, tap, tap . . .

I needed to get up from the table, but couldn't move. John Wu, Carlos, and Jason looked around like this was fun. Like it was some kind of joke.

The table rose about an inch off the ground, and then I heard it.

The beast. The growl.

Grrrrrrrr.

Grrrrrrrrrrrrrrrrr.

No, no, NO!

This couldn't be happening right now. Not during lunch. Not in front of the whole school. Did the creature follow us here?

Was I dreaming?

That was it. I was dreaming because there was no way Shelby would ever admit to not knowing something.

Bryant pushed his chair away with a scream.

I could hardly breathe. After one last loud growl, the

table slammed down and a familiar puff of red hair emerged from under the table.

Shelby!!!

She had a smug look on her face as she held up her phone. "Well, Watson, I think I have an explanation for the noises."

"Shelby!" I hissed. I couldn't believe she hid under the table to scare us. She practically gave me a heart attack! And Bryant looked like he was about to faint. "Bryant, are you okay? I'm really sorry about that."

"That was cool!" Carlos exclaimed, completely oblivious to how rattled Bryant was (not to mention me). "Hey, Shelby, can you help us with our Halloween costumes?"

"You really should consider being part of the tech group for the plays, Shelby," John Wu said with admiration in his voice. "You'd kill it with special effects."

Bryant glared at Shelby. "Is this a joke to you?"

"Oh, you're fine." Shelby paused for a moment and took in a red-faced Bryant. "Relatively speaking. I'm simply trying to help."

"I don't need your help," Bryant said through gritted teeth.

Shelby folded her arms. "Your demeanor and lack of explanation for what's happening with your apartment building say otherwise."

I pulled Shelby to the side, my hands jittering from

nerves. "I can't believe you did that! You know how unsettled we are. That wasn't funny, Shelby."

She shrugged. "It was a little funny."

"Shelby! It was mean."

She recoiled slightly at that. "I was merely trying to make a point."

"You could've done that without scaring us half to death," I scolded her quietly. "Plus, the apartment where the noise was coming from was *empty*. There wasn't anybody hiding, playing some mean trick."

Shelby grimaced. "Okay. I could've warned you. My apologies. However, I did it because I wanted to prove that you can fool people into thinking something is haunted. You being privy to that information ahead of time wouldn't have had the same result, but yes, it was perhaps a bit too dramatic after the night you've had. I've been thinking about what you experienced, and I believe this case is worthy enough of my talents."

There was no way Bryant was going to have her help us now. No. Way.

I promised him she wouldn't make fun of him. Shelby did that on top of causing a scene in front of the entire cafeteria.

This was not cool.

But—and I had to admit it—we needed Shelby's help.

And she knew it.

"Hold on and just try to not upset anybody for two minutes." I turned away from Shelby and approached Bryant.

I took a deep breath before I placed my hand lightly on his shoulder. "I'm sorry, man." Bryant glared at Shelby across from the table where she was eating a cookie like it was a typical Tuesday for her. "That was awful and unacceptable and mean and, well, I told Shelby as much. You have every right to be mad at her, because I am, too."

"I told you." Bryant's face was crimson with fear or anger or embarrassment, or possibly all three.

"I know. She was trying to prove something. Not the way I would've done it," I admitted. "She was able to make us believe that the table was haunted. Listen, you have issues with Shelby—believe me, I do on most days. She may know how this is happening and can help us find the person responsible for this."

Bryant looked surprised. "What do you mean? You think someone is doing this to mess with us?"

"I don't know. That's the problem. *I don't know.* I couldn't explain anything that was happening last night, but Shelby will be able to. We need her."

Bryant looked down at the floor for a moment. When he finally looked up it was clear he wasn't happy. But he knew we were in over our heads. "Only if she apologizes for what she did." Bryant folded his arms.

"Yeah, sure," I said, even though that was easier said than done. "Shelby, come over here."

Shelby strolled over. "Yes, can I help with something?"

Aw man, she was going to make this difficult. Of course she would!

"First, you need to say you're sorry."

"You're sorry," she repeated with a snort.

"Shelby," I warned her, "remember our talk."

Shelby sulked for a moment before she pulled her shoulders back. "My sincerest apologies that you frighten so easily, Bryant."

"Shelby!"

"I realize you've been under great strain, so I shouldn't have done it." She glared at me the entire time she was giving this so-called apology, but Bryant should have realized this was as good as he was going to get. "Is that all?"

Bryant let out a loud groan. "No, um, Shelby?"

"Yes." Shelby smiled sweetly at him, which just infuriated Bryant even more.

He looked like he was in physical pain. "Can you come over to my apartment after school?"

"Why, Bryant, I thought you'd never ask."

⌐·CHAPTER·⌐
7

SHELBY AND I HAD TO HAVE THE TALK.

Again.

"Can you please try to be nice to Bryant?" I begged as we waited for Bryant at my locker after school. "That stunt you pulled in the cafeteria was really mean."

"So you've previously informed me, and I have apologized," she replied with a dismissive sniff.

"Shelby, please. Bryant is one of our clients now."

"Watson, I am always professional with our clients. I believe it would be rather impossible to name one client who wasn't satisfied with my results." She turned her nose up at me.

Yeah, I'd never argue that our clients weren't happy when we solved a case, but Shelby could never be considered friendly. Besides, this was the first time one of our clients was one of my friends. A friend, no less, who really, really, really didn't like Shelby.

Really, *really*.

Time to try a different approach. If she wasn't going to do me a favor, at least I could reason with her.

Or so I'd hope.

"You know how I was this morning?"

Shelby tilted her head. "I do recall your abrupt temperament."

Um, seriously? Shelby was commenting on someone else's *abrupt temperament*.

"Yeah, I was tired and out of sorts because I had a horrible night's sleep. Well, Bryant has had three nights like that. In his own house. So try to put yourself in his shoes and tread carefully. What we need right now is to assure him that we're going to figure this out and that he has nothing to worry about. No more tricks."

Shelby huffed. "Do you want me to solve this, or do you want me to be well behaved?"

"Can't you do both?"

Her face turned up in such a scowl, I should've known better than to ask her that question.

"It's for a friend of mine," I added. Yeah, she and Bryant might not get along, but he and I did. It's the least Shelby could do for me after all I put up with being her partner. "You do things for your friends. I'd do whatever you needed. That's what friends do: they help each other."

"I don't need help," Shelby said with a clenched jaw.

Here's the thing: sometimes the great Shelby Holmes did need help. She didn't always understand how to behave around people, even if she wouldn't admit it. I tried to guide her in the right direction, especially when it came to our clients.

"Yeah, but some people do. Bryant needs our help. Friend to friend, can you please play nice?"

"I'll try," she relented. "For you, Watson."

That was going to have to be good enough.

"Although," Shelby started, and I had to know it wasn't going to be that simple. "You infer that I'm the only friend being difficult, yet have you ever thought about my point of view?"

That stopped me in my tracks.

Shelby continued, "Have you not observed how Bryant constantly glares at me? You're not in our music class to see how agitated he gets when I'm asked to play a piece to demonstrate the proper technique. I'm able to put all of that aside to work on his case, so he should do the same."

Shelby had a point. I never really thought about how people treated her since I was usually too busy trying to make up for her behavior. It was true: nobody really talked to her unless they needed her help. That wasn't fair to Shelby.

"I'm sorry—" I began to apologize, but Shelby cut me off.

"Watson, it is the reality of my school existence. This is why I don't like to make any case personal or get involved with clients and suspects. Bryant's case is one that has intrigued me. So I'll work on it. I'll play nice, but I'm solely doing it for you."

"Thanks, Shelby."

"Besides, friends seem to only take up time and bring a lot of dramatics to life, so I'm content with my current situation."

Ah, I think her current situation meant me. Yeah, Shelby could be a lot and that stunt she did in the cafeteria still wasn't cool, but she was human. And my friend.

Bryant came toward us down the hallway, a look of apprehension on his face. Shelby straightened up and attempted what I could only assume was a welcoming smile. Between the strain of her lips and the narrowing of her eyes, it looked as if the simple gesture of a smile was causing her pain.

Still, she was trying.

"Hey," Bryant greeted us. He kicked the floor. "I, ah, got this for you, Shelby." Bryant reached into his jacket pocket and pulled out a candy bar.

Oh! There may be hope for these two yet.

Shelby's face lit up with genuine happiness this time. "Splendid!" She unwrapped the candy bar as we began to walk out of school. "Bryant, this could be the start of a beautiful acquaintance."

Shelby had an extra skip in her step while we walked to Bryant's apartment. Once the candy bar was finished (so, like, 2.4 seconds later), quiet descended on the group. It was awkward. I nudged Shelby. Bryant was nice enough to get her something, so it was now her turn to attempt to be civil to him.

"Bryant, your martelé has much improved."

I had no idea what that meant, but Bryant seemed suspicious at Shelby's now friendly behavior. "Ah, okay."

"I'm being serious. You must have been working on it."

"I have," Bryant said as he walked just a tad taller.

"I can tell." Shelby then nodded at me. No doubt she wanted me to acknowledge that she could be human every once in a while.

"Thanks," Bryant replied. "So are you going to use one of those EMF meters?"

Shelby looked confused. "Are you referring to an electromagnetic field meter? Why on earth would I use that?"

She then did a full-on witchlike cackle.

So Shelby and Bryant on friendly terms lasted ten seconds. Better than I expected.

"It's a reasonable question!" Bryant whipped his shaggy hair back. "It's what people use on ghost shows."

"Ghost shows? Like a cartoon?" Shelby's face scrunched up in disgust.

Oh, come on. I made a note to ask Shelby's parents about what cartoons Shelby watched as a kid, because there was no way she hadn't watched a Disney movie or owned a stuffed animal. Just no way.

Sure, the Holmeses didn't appear to have a television in any of the rooms that I'd been in, but they could watch stuff on computers.

"No, it's a reality show"—Shelby snorted, but Bryant continued—"where people go to haunted houses to find ghosts. And the Ghostbusters used EMFs, too."

Shelby clenched her jaw a moment before taking a deep breath. "Electromagnetic field meters would certainly diagnose any electrical currents. Why they'd use one on those so-called reality shows is beyond me. Dare I even inquire who these Ghostbusters are?"

"You know, the ones from the movies?"

Shelby looked at Bryant blankly.

I shook my head at him. "Shelby doesn't really watch movies. Or TV."

Bryant's jaw dropped. "Really?"

Shelby shrugged. "I prefer to use my imagination while reading books instead of the passive entertainment you lot seem to favor."

I gave Shelby a warning look. Plus, movies and TV shows were awesome. I liked books, too. People could like more than one thing.

An idea occurred to me. Maybe, just maybe, we could learn a few things from watching one of those ghost-hunting shows. Not sure how I was going to convince Shelby of that, but she had her ways of researching, and I had mine.

We turned onto Bryant's street and saw a group of people outside the building. They were looking up at the Baskerville Estates sign and taking pictures.

"Is this a normal occurrence outside your building?" Shelby asked as she rubbed her hands together.

"No," Bryant replied.

"Did something happen?" I asked with dread in my voice.

"No, it's a tour group," Shelby stated. "Look at the people: comfortable walking shoes, various clothing accoutrements to show where they're from, cameras dangling or pointed at the building. There are certainly a number of historical and city walking tours in Harlem. Does your building have any historic significance?"

"Not that I know of," Bryant said. "I've never seen a tour group outside our building before."

Shelby smiled. "Interesting. It appears the ruse is on."

Before she could explain more, Shelby started walking

toward the group. A white guy in his early twenties, dressed in all black, with heavy black eyeliner, led a group consisting of about a dozen tourists who were rapt with attention.

The guide dramatically swept his hand to the building. "This year marks the one-hundredth anniversary of when Hugo Baskerville met his untimely demise. Every year around Halloween, residents hear Hugo pacing around the building and the cries of his beloved hound. Legend has it that the soul of Hugo Baskerville will not rest until he can find peace in the home he so loved."

Yikes. Bryant's apartment building really was haunted! And it was famous!

But . . . Bryant had lived there for years. Mr. Mortimer has been there even longer. If this really was a haunting, why now? The anniversary? A hundred years did seem like a big deal, even for ghosts.

Yeah, Shelby said that there was no such thing as ghosts and that she could figure out what was going on. But she still hadn't proved it wasn't a haunting, so I was going to proceed with caution.

Just a day in and this case was throwing me for a loop. I'd get ready to think one thing, and then something else would change my mind.

"Question!" Shelby said with her hand raised. She had inserted herself in the tour group. "We have sadly only

caught the tail end of your presentation about this building. Are you giving another tour soon?"

"Yes!" the guide said. "Every day during the week of Halloween, as that is when Hugo Baskerville makes his appearance."

"So it's only this building on this tour?"

"No, it's haunted areas of Harlem," the tour guide said in a deep voice that got louder with each word. "But if you're interested in the legend of Hugo Baskerville, I have more information."

Shelby took the brochure from the guy. "I was certain you would."

"Now!" he exclaimed as he clapped his hands. "This is the time to take pictures of the building. Hugo lived in the apartment on the third floor, the two windows to the right." He pointed at the windows directly above where Bryant and his mom lived.

Uh-oh.

It was official: I was creeped out.

Shelby didn't even glance at the piece of paper before handing it to me. It was a photocopy of an old *New York Times* article from November 2, 1919, featuring two pictures: one of the front of Bryant's apartment building and one of a white guy with one of those old-timey handlebar mustaches. Bryant looked over my shoulder as I read it.

REAL ESTATE MAGNATE HUGO BASKERVILLE MURDERED!

By Mara I. Rhody

Infamous real estate tycoon Hugo Baskerville was found murdered in his eponymous building in Harlem. A tenant in the Baskerville Estates alerted police when Baskerville's beloved hound kept barking through the night. Authorities discovered the hound guarding Baskerville's bloodied and lifeless body. Baskerville was bludgeoned to death by an unknown object.

Baskerville, a trendsetter in building during the Harlem Renaissance, had recently been accused of scamming his tenants. Could it be a tenant who snapped? Residents of the building are currently being interviewed for any information leading to the capture of the murderer.

Baskerville's hound has refused to leave the apartment since the murder on Halloween and continues to howl through the night.

Murder! I didn't know he was MURDERED. I mean, dying was bad enough, but MURDER.

Nope. I was done. Out. And I wasn't ashamed.

Before I could admit this to Shelby, she turned to the tour guide.

"Excuse me," Shelby cooed, which only meant one thing: this guy was in trouble. "I don't mean to interrupt as I'm sure you have various other locales to show, but I'm Jenna Lee Miller. My mother is *the* Joanne Miller from Miller Casting. I think you have a wonderful presence about you that would be perfect for a television show she's currently working on. Do you have your head shot on you?"

The dude's dark eyes got wide. "Yes!" he said in a chipper voice, very different from the somber tone he'd been using during his tour. "Listen, your mom is one of the best casting agents. I'd love for her to have my credentials!" He reached into his messenger bag and pulled out a glossy photo of himself—without the eye makeup and slicked-back hair—and with text on the back.

"Wonderful," Shelby purred. "Thank you so much."

He gave her a big smile before he turned back to the group in a dour manner.

Shelby looked like she'd won something.

I was as confused as ever. "What was that? How do you know a casting director?"

"I don't."

"But he knew about her."

Shelby turned to Bryant. "I didn't realize the great violin maestro Leonardo Pileggio lived down the street from you."

Bryant snapped out of his fog. "Oh, yeah."

"Have you had the pleasure of conversing with him?"

What on earth did this have to do with this case? AND A MURDER!

Bryant nodded. "A little. I don't want to bother him."

"How considerate of you." Shelby turned back to me. "People often pretend to know something in order to not feel foolish. Case in point: I made up Leonardo Pileggio, but Bryant wouldn't want me to think he wasn't aware of some great violin maestro, especially one who lived nearby."

Bryant looked like a deer caught in headlights.

Shelby continued, "That guide wasn't some horror expert. He was an actor. While you were reading that sham of an article, I asked him basic questions about Hugo Baskerville, and he stuttered. He stated that Hugo was born in 1912, which would've meant that he was seven at the time of his alleged murder. Actor? Yes. Good at improvisation? No."

"What are you saying?" I asked. So the guide was an actor. Big deal. I was pretty sure half the waiters in this city were actors. That didn't mean anything.

Right?

"It signifies that this web is getting quite intricate, and I

63

love a good puzzle." Shelby patted Bryant on the shoulder. "Buck up, Bryant. This is getting fun!"

"Fun?" Bryant said in a hushed tone. "How is any of this fun?"

"Yeah, about that," I tried to explain. "Shelby's idea of what's fun is very different from most people's."

Bryant gulped. "No kidding."

Shelby clapped her hands excitedly. "Now let's go inside!"

CHAPTER 8

IF I THOUGHT IT WAS AWKWARD WHEN WE WERE WALKING here, it was nothing compared to Shelby being in Bryant's apartment.

She immediately began crawling on the floor. She examined every crevice of the windows along the street side of the apartment before turning her attention to the living room–dining room–kitchen. Her eyes never more than an inch away from any surface.

"Ah, Watson," Bryant began. "What's she doing?"

"It's just this thing she does," I replied. I had no idea *why* she was doing it, but I knew to never question her methods.

Shelby jumped up from the floor. She dusted off her knees, then clapped her hands. "Now to the bathroom and bedrooms."

Bryant didn't look happy. "Why? Nothing has happened there. Is it necessary?"

"Yes, I need to understand every inch of this apartment to deduce how this is transpiring."

Bryant reluctantly led us to the back of the apartment. First Shelby inspected the bathroom and Bryant's mom's room—under Bryant's watchful and untrusting eye—before turning to Bryant's room.

"Oh, come on!" Bryant groaned as Shelby looked under his bed.

"Nothing's in there!" he protested as she opened his closet.

"Unbelievable!" he said with a sigh as she opened his dresser. "I guess privacy means nothing to you?"

I was pretty certain Shelby went over Bryant's bedroom more closely. She was storing information in her brain attic about him. I just knew it.

"Can you be careful with that?" Bryant said as Shelby picked up his violin.

"I believe I am more than equipped to handle this instrument," she said with a dismissive sniff.

Shelby went over to his small wooden desk and moved it around.

"What are you looking for?" I asked, hoping to ease Bryant's nerves and, you know, also clue me in on what was going on.

"I'll know when I find it."

Yep. That was Shelby being super open about her process. To her partner. Because that's to be expected.

"Do you really need to do that?" Bryant asked while Shelby started opening his desk drawers.

"You want answers? I'm trying to get them."

"Yeah, but, I mean—" Bryant started before Shelby smirked as she picked up a teddy bear dressed as a Mets fan, Bryant's favorite team. "Okay! That's enough!" He grabbed the bear from her and held it tightly to his chest. "Tour's over."

"Yeah, Shelby," I agreed. "I think you got enough information here." I gave her that look that hopefully said *remember what I said about playing nice.*

"Not yet." Shelby pulled out her cell phone. "It is quite difficult to decipher infrasound because the human ear cannot detect it, which is the issue. I haven't identified anything that could potentially emit an infrasound. I could put sheets of acrylic plastic on the windows as it would respond to infrasound, but that wouldn't let us know where it was coming from. So this is the next best thing."

She stood on Bryant's bed—despite his protest—with her phone held out, going over every surface on the wall, focusing on the vent. She then worked her way back through the apartment.

As she was standing in the middle of Bryant's shower, he finally had enough. "What are you doing with your phone?"

"I'm using a condenser mic that is connected to an A/D converter, which can capture low frequencies as digital signals."

Bryant held up his hands. "Never mind. Sorry I asked."

I gave him an understanding pat on the back. *I know, I know . . .*

After going over every surface in the apartment for a second time, first with her eyes, second with whatever microphone thingy she rigged up on her phone, Shelby stopped.

She looked confused. She reached into her pocket and pulled out a bag of M&M's. She poured half of the bag into her mouth before closing her eyes.

This meant Shelby was stumped. So, not a good sign.

"No infrasound?" I asked.

Shelby shook her head.

Yep, this wasn't good at all. AT. ALL.

Because if it wasn't this sound that was causing the ghost-like feelings in the tenants of the building, what was it?

Yep. Like I said before, I was out. I signed up with Shelby to find dogs and cipher-sending bullies. Not to get involved in something where a murder was involved. Even one that was nearly a century old.

Nope.

Bryant gulped. "So, it's really Baskerville's ghost?"

He backed away from Shelby. It seemed like he might run depending on what her answer was.

Shelby snorted. "It should go without saying that it is not a ghost."

That dismissive answer from Shelby didn't relax Bryant. To be honest, it didn't convince me, either.

"So now what?" I asked. How were we going to solve a case that we couldn't see?

Because as much as I wanted to abandon Baskerville Estates—again, MURDER—I'd never do that to Bryant. But, well, I was too embarrassed to admit to Shelby that I was scared. So yeah, I was not feeling really great about myself then.

Shelby smirked. "Bryant, it's time I meet your neighbors."

"My neighbors? Why?"

"This is clearly an inside job."

CHAPTER 9

"WHAT?" BRYANT EXCLAIMED. "WHAT DO YOU MEAN, 'INSIDE job'? You think a neighbor is responsible for this?"

"Absolutely," Shelby replied in a way that made it seem like she was shocked that neither Bryant nor I had thought of it first. "To even enter this building requires two keys for two different locks: one for the first door, a second for the door after the mailboxes. The lock on the inside door is a Complex Key Lock X14, which is very difficult to pick. It takes me nearly two minutes to crack, and I'm quite fast when it comes to picking locks."

Bryant made the wise decision to sit down on his couch at this point. He'd never been that impressed whenever I'd talk about the cases Shelby and I worked on. Now, as he saw Shelby in action, he knew she was something else.

Shelby continued, "It would take someone picking locks too long to enter the building, especially with your landlord living on the first floor, with his door only four and a half feet away from the main door."

"Wait." Bryant put his hands on his head. "How do you know how far away it is?"

"I observe. I presume you've never noticed."

Bryant fell back on the couch.

"You've at least had to observe the person in your building who smokes."

Bryant perked back up. "What? Smoking isn't allowed in our apartments. Mr. Barrymore is very strict about that. No smoking and no pets."

"That doesn't mean someone in this building doesn't smoke. She simply chooses to do it outside. It's a young woman. Who fits that description?"

Bryant shook his head. "I don't under—" He took a deep breath. "How do you know this?"

"Since you were unaware of the distance between doors, I'll assume that you haven't observed the discarded cigarette butts in the nook adjacent to your building. The ones with traces of lipstick."

Bryant's jaw was open. "That could be anybody."

"Since it's a location in which one exiting the building wouldn't be seen, it is an excellent hiding space. Therefore, I deduce it's a teenage girl. Her parents or parent aren't aware she does it."

"You can't mean Kaitlin?" He shook his head. "Kaitlin is a junior in high school and lives with her mom upstairs. She doesn't smoke."

"I believe I have proven she does. I would like to get a word with her. While I do not approve of such a filthy habit, it does mean she spends a lot of time outside the building. She should make a good witness."

"I don't smell cigarette smoke on her."

"Fabric spray, mints, mouthwash, holding the cigarette away from you to not have the smoke linger on your person. It's fairly easy to hide it from people who aren't observant, especially if her mother is anything like the rest of the tenants in this building."

Shelby let that insult hang in the air.

As much as I wanted to scold her for being so rude, Shelby did have a point. (It was always so irritating when she was right.)

"Shall we?" Shelby said as she extended her arm to the door.

"Well, I guess we'll start with Mr. Mortimer across the hall," Bryant suggested. "Ms. Lyons and Kaitlin won't be home for a little while. Ms. Lyons is a teacher down in the Upper West Side, so she gets home closer to four. Mr. Mortimer is usually home."

We walked across the hall and knocked on apartment 2. I could hear the sound of a TV through the door.

The door opened, and Mr. Mortimer looked at the three of us. "Who are your friends, John?"

Bryant pointed to me. "This is John Watson and *his* friend, Shelby Holmes."

If Bryant refusing to refer to Shelby as his friend bothered her, she didn't show it. Shelby didn't get upset about being left out of things. She wanted to sit alone at lunch. Things like friends were an inconvenience to her.

Sigh . . .

"Do you mind if we ask you some questions?" Shelby asked before her attention went to the TV. It was some true crime show. The narrator's voice boomed, "How can this case be solved only by a letter?"

Shelby rolled her eyes. "A letter is a perfect way to solve a case. There's ample DNA on an envelope that's licked. Fairly straightforward." She turned to me. "Do people really watch these mundane programs?"

Mr. Mortimer adjusted his glasses before chuckling. "You seem pretty smart, young lady."

"Smart is an understatement," Shelby replied in her oh-so-modest way. "Can you tell us about any weird feelings or occurrences you've experienced in the last few days? Any weird noises."

"My hearing isn't what it used to be." He tapped on his hearing aid. "But I've heard that dang dog barking up a storm at night. Lived in this building forty years. Never had a problem. Neighbors aren't like they used to be. No respect. All that incessant babbling, walking up and down the stairs. Don't get me started on the racket when the ladies above me insist on wearing those high-heeled shoes."

"Any strange sensations?" Shelby pressed.

"Young lady, when you get to be my age, they're all strange sensations." He chuckled some more before he began to cough. A lot. "This dang cough is going to be the death of me." He reached into his pocket and pulled out a cough drop.

"Did you know that in Germany, thyme is an officially approved cough treatment, even for upper respiratory infections? Steep two teaspoons in a cup of boiling water. If you don't have any thyme, Bryant has some in his kitchen in the far upper-right cabinet."

Mr. Mortimer looked impressed. "Is there anything you don't know?"

"I know everything of importance," Shelby said, which made him laugh—and cough —more.

We heard footsteps coming up the stairs. A white woman in her late forties walked up the stairs with a teenage girl behind her. Both had auburn hair. The infamous Kaitlin and her mom, I presumed?

"Hey, Ms. Lyons," Bryant said with a nod. "Do you think we can talk to you guys for a minute about all the stuff happening in the building? These are my friends. And well, they know a lot of things and can help us."

Got to admit, my chest puffed up a bit with that comment. Sure, I didn't know as much as Shelby, but I could hold my own. Hadn't done it so far with this case, but it seemed that I had plenty of time to figure something out. Anything.

"Please, come on up," Ms. Lyons replied.

"Thanks, Mr. Mortimer. Feel better," I said with a small wave.

"I hope you guys find that blasted dog!" he commented before closing his door.

"Watson," Shelby said as we climbed the stairs to the third floor. "I need you to distract Ms. Lyons so I can question Kaitlin alone. I don't have the time or the patience to play around with how I have knowledge that she's the one who spends time outside the building. So I must be blunt and get straight to it."

"Yeah, but how do I—"

"We've lived here five years," Ms. Lyons started as she opened up her apartment for us. The five of us crowded around the small kitchen table. "It's been a good home, but lately . . ."

"Yeah, maybe we'll finally move now," Kaitlin said as she typed on her phone. "I've been begging to move to Brooklyn for forever so I can be closer to my friends."

"And as I keep telling you: Brooklyn is too far of a commute for me. We're not moving so you can be closer to some boy."

"You mean it's too far away from Thomas." Kaitlin pretended to gag.

"We're not having this conversation again," Ms. Lyons snapped at Kaitlin before turning her attention to us.

"Thomas Stapleton is our upstairs neighbor and a dear, dear friend. As I was saying, we've had no issues, but now . . . it's surreal. And a little unsettling." She rubbed her tired face.

I glanced over at Shelby, who was glaring at me. So I guess she meant it that she didn't want to waste any time, even to be polite.

Oh, right, Shelby Holmes didn't do polite. My bad.

Okay, I needed to get Ms. Lyons talking about something to get her distracted so Shelby could pull Kaitlin aside. And . . . I was drawing a blank.

Then Shelby's most often quoted piece of advice sprang in my head: *Don't simply see, observe.*

I looked around the apartment. Every wall surface was covered with framed posters of Broadway shows.

Bingo!

I walked up to one of the posters and said, "My mom and I moved here a few months ago and we haven't seen any Broadway shows. Is this one good?"

Ms. Lyons walked over to me. "You must go immediately! There is nothing like live theater. I prefer musicals. I see everything when it comes out, *everything*. I even saw *Hamilton* with its original cast."

"Impressive," I replied, since her tone indicated that should be the reply. See, Shelby wasn't the only one who could make deductions! "So it's good?"

Well, that did it. Ms. Lyons started talking excitedly about the show. She gave me a wink when she told me that a black actor played George Washington. Which I had to admit was pretty cool. Then, she, ah, um . . . rapped. Why this woman was rapping to me about not throwing away her shot, I have no idea. Got to admit, she wasn't that bad. For a white woman. At this point, the dreaded hound could start howling and she wouldn't have noticed.

Mission accomplished. Hey, I hadn't been hanging out with Shelby Holmes for nothing.

After I'd heard about Ms. Lyons's top-ten musicals of all time and then the three shows Mom and I must see *immediately*, Shelby approached to thank her for having us over. She didn't look that excited or smug, so I deduced that Kaitlin didn't have any useful intel.

Once the door closed behind us, Shelby groaned. "You know the problem, well, one, with young people these days? They are always on their phones. Staring at a screen instead of observing anything around them."

"Are you referring to Kaitlin?" I asked. You know, the "young person" who was probably six or seven years older than Shelby.

Shelby replied by grimacing. So that was that, I guessed.

"Although she could be lying as she has a very powerful motive."

"Wait," I said as I started to put it together. "You think she's doing this so they'll move?"

"It's a possibility."

"Kaitlin?" Bryant looked shocked. "I don't think she'd do that."

"You also didn't think she smoked," Shelby fired back.

Point to Shelby.

Shelby looked up the flight of stairs. "And this Thomas Stapleton Ms. Lyons mentioned lives above them on the top floor?"

"Yeah," Bryant answered. "But he's hardly around. He travels a lot for work. He left for a business trip the day before the noise started."

"And in the other apartment?"

"Oh, no. There's only one apartment upstairs. It used to be two, but Stapleton converted it when the last tenant left a couple years ago. Mr. Barrymore's uncle was more than happy for him to do it since Stapleton paid for the conversion himself."

"And why would your landlord's uncle have an opinion on the matter?"

"Oh." Bryant's shoulders slumped for a moment. "The first Mr. Barrymore—the uncle—was our landlord before he passed away. His nephew, Jay, inherited the apartment building."

"I see," Shelby said as she looked down the stairs. "How long ago was that?"

"About two years."

Shelby nodded. "Well, I guess we must talk to the current Mr. Barrymore. It is also imperative we see this apartment." She pointed to the door across from the Lyonses'. The one where the noise was coming from.

Hmm, I wondered if I could get out of that tour.

We walked down to the first floor. I focused on the space between Barrymore's door and the front one. I couldn't tell you if it was in fact four and a half feet, but I knew if I had a ruler it would be an exact match.

Barrymore opened the door. It made sense he inherited the building. He looked too young to be a landlord. I'd guess midtwenties. "Hey, John, how's everything? The apartment okay?"

"Yeah, but we have some questions for you."

After Bryant made the introductions since Mr. Barrymore was too busy last night trying to figure out the noise to meet me, he welcomed us into his apartment. Even though it was bigger than Bryant's above, as it took up the entire first floor, it was cluttered with boxes. Instead of a couch in the living room, there was an old wooden desk next to several metal file cabinets.

"Do you live here?" Shelby asked.

"Yeah, I use the second bedroom as a living room. It was

easier to clean all that out instead of this—" He gestured to what had to be decades' worth of paperwork.

"And how long has this building been in your family?"

Mr. Barrymore rubbed his chin. "Since the forties, I think. My grandfather bought it, and then my uncle Randall took it over. And when Uncle Randall passed away . . . well, I was the only family member still in the area. I spent so much time here as a kid. I even lived in apartment six when I was in grade school."

"So you're a landlord on top of being a grad student at Columbia and interning?"

Barrymore wasn't the only one who did a double take. I scanned the apartment to see if I could piece together how Shelby knew this. A few business textbooks and a Columbia Business School MBA coffee mug sat on the desk. I made a mental note to start observing the second I walked into an apartment so I could beat Shelby at her own game, just once.

"Yes," Mr. Barrymore said. "It was really great for Uncle Randall to leave me the apartment building in his will, because it's helped pay for grad school and allowed me to get an internship. The landlord gig wasn't something that took up too much time, until recently."

Hmm. There was something off when Mr. Barrymore talked. He kept shifting his feet and looking around the apartment instead of making eye contact. Maybe the inheritance wasn't so fortunate after all.

But then again, he could've just sold the building if he didn't want it. And everybody needed a place to live.

So maybe he was a possible suspect, but who knew at this point? I guess all signs pointed to Kaitlin? Although Shelby said never to guess.

"Do you recall who your family bought the building from?"

Barrymore nodded. "Yeah. When all the stuff started happening, I looked up the history. Franklin Baskerville sold it to my grandfather. The guy who built this building was his uncle, Hugo."

"I'm sensing a theme," Shelby said with a snort.

"I just . . ." Barrymore sighed. "This building hasn't had so much as a pipe burst in the time I've been here, and now all of a sudden . . . I'd heard the stories about this building being cursed when I was little, but I'd assumed it was just a way to scare me."

Shelby scoffed. "Cursed? Are you referring to this nonsense about Hugo Baskerville's ghost?"

Barrymore nodded solemnly. "Whenever something would go bump in the night, my dad would joke about the Baskerville curse. He'd tell me about freaky things happening around Halloween, but I didn't believe it until this past weekend."

Shelby pinched her lips together like she was getting ready to laugh.

I was totally lost if this was some kind of joke. Because there was nothing funny about murder and curses.

MURDER AND CURSES!

As much as Shelby said this was an inside job, there was no denying that Hugo Baskerville was a real person and his ghost was famous.

What were we even still doing in this building?

"May we see apartment five?" Shelby asked.

It was like she could read my mind. Because of course she wanted us to go into the apartment that was haunted.

My stomach dropped. It didn't matter what Shelby said. She wasn't here last night. She didn't hear the noise.

So yeah, it was quiet now. I didn't have that same dreaded feeling, either. Maybe it was because it was still light out. Barely. Were we going to be in that apartment when it got dark?

Because *no thank you* if we were. I planned to stay near the door and bolt if anything happened. There was no shame in wanting to protect yourself. None.

As we started to climb back up the stairs, Mr. Barrymore explained that the new tenant kept pushing back his move-in date. "But he keeps paying rent, so no complaints from me!"

Bryant was standing behind me as Barrymore began unlocking the door. It took two locks with two different keys to open. So if someone was coming in and picking locks, there'd be four locks in total. Shelby was onto something. It had to be someone here. One of the neighbors could have made copies of the keys to this apartment. The Holmeses have a set of our keys in case we got locked out and our landlady, Mrs. Hudson, wasn't around. Not like Shelby couldn't simply pick our lock. (Which she did once, but I can't even get into that story. She was truly unbelievable. Truly.)

The door opened to the apartment, and it was . . . empty.

I felt myself relax a bit. There was nothing scary at all. It was exactly like Bryant's apartment. It somehow looked smaller without furniture in it. Shelby got on all fours and started examining every crevice while I walked around.

Huh. As I walked, I felt off. It was hard to describe. I simply didn't feel balanced.

Maybe it was the power of suggestion. Or maybe it was something else.

Bryant put his hand on the wall to steady himself after taking a few steps.

So I wasn't imagining it.

I was about to bring it to Shelby's attention when out of nowhere the door to the apartment slammed shut.

Bryant screamed. At first I thought it was from the sound of the door.

But no.

How I wished it was only that.

Shelby could explain away feelings and sounds, but this—this was real. And it was absolutely terrifying.

There on the inside of the door were giant claw marks.

CHAPTER 10

Out! Out! Out!

I don't mind admitting that I took off down the stairs so I could exit that crazy haunted building. And it wasn't just me. Bryant went first. I followed him down with Mr. Barrymore close on my heels.

All I wanted to do was to breathe fresh air. This building was too much.

"What's going on?" Ms. Lyons called after us.

"We're not safe!" Bryant yelled as we fled through the front door.

Ms. Lyons and Kaitlin joined us in front of the building. The five of us were breathless and out of sorts.

Want to know who stayed in there?

Yep. Shelby.

Of course she did.

"What happened? What's going on?" Ms. Lyons asked, her voice getting higher.

"I—I—I'm not sure," Mr. Barrymore stuttered.

Neither was I. But I knew my eyes were not deceiving me. There were definitely claw marks on that door. Those of a big beast. A very, *very* big beast.

"Mr. Mortimer is still in there!" Bryant exclaimed.

We all looked around at each other, wondering who was going to be brave enough to go back in there and get him.

The front door swung open and out waltzed Shelby, as calm as could be. She even had a lollipop in her mouth.

"What was it?" Bryant asked her, a quiver in his voice.

Shelby removed the red lollipop and held it out to make a point. "It wasn't from a giant beast, I can tell you that much."

Nobody seemed to believe her. Including me.

"Giant beast?" Ms. Lyons exclaimed. "What giant beast? Did you see that . . . that *thing* we've been hearing?"

Everyone was focused on Shelby . . . except Kaitlin, who stared down at her phone. Shelby was right. She'd make a horrible witness.

"No, we did not see the imaginary beast," said Shelby. "On the inside door there were fake claw marks."

Shelby held up a piece of paper that had the claw marks outlined by rubbing a pencil over them.

"Fake?" I knew at this point that Shelby was careful with the words she used.

She handed me the piece of paper. "Yes. They weren't from any animal."

"How do you know?" Bryant asked.

"Watson?" Shelby said to me.

I looked at the straight, exact marks from the outline. *Oh wow.* I saw it. If I'd maybe stayed in the apartment instead of fleeing, I would've noticed it, too.

"These marks are too precise," I replied. "Each mark is the exact same length and perfectly straight. Dogs' paws, and their nails, aren't straight, just like human hands." I pulled in my pinkie and thumb to show them my three inside fingers. "If I was to scratch something, the middle finger would be higher."

Shelby nodded in approval and it felt just as great as you could imagine.

Shelby crossed her arms. "Yes, I'll have to experiment on Sir Arthur later tonight to confirm my suspicions. However, I do believe it was done with a handheld cultivator."

"A what?"

Shelby sighed. "It is a basic garden tool."

Everybody else was at a loss for words.

"Sir Arthur is Shelby's English bulldog," I explained. "We'll have him claw something so we can see if we're right."

Shelby scoffed at my insinuation that we could be wrong. I mean, I get why she'd be annoyed, but I needed to explain to them what was going on.

Wait, so if someone left this with a garden tool that meant it wasn't haunted.

But then why did I feel uneasy in that room?

"I'm texting Antonio to tell him I'm staying at his place tonight," Kaitlin remarked as her fingers worked overtime.

"No, you will not!" Ms. Lyons exclaimed. "I'll figure something else out."

Kaitlin threw her head back and groaned. "You never listen to me!" she shouted before stomping down the street.

Ms. Lyons pinched the bridge of her nose. "I hate to say it, but Kaitlin has a point about wanting to stay somewhere else. And, John, I'm certain when your mother comes home she'll feel the same way. It's not safe until we know exactly what is happening. Noises are one thing, but claw marks are another."

"No, please," Mr. Barrymore said as he approached her cautiously. "I understand you're upset, but this place has been my family's home for decades. It's safe. You're safe."

But he didn't even seem to convince himself.

"You are safe," Shelby confirmed. "As I believe Watson and I have proven, there were no claw marks. I need to do some research, but I'm certain I'll have some answers tomorrow."

"I'm going to call Thomas to fill him in on what's happening," Ms. Lyons said. "Maybe he'll have some ideas."

She walked off to the side and took out her phone.

"I guess I'll go check in on Mr. Mortimer," Mr. Barrymore said before heading back into the building.

"Interesting," Shelby said as she studied Ms. Lyons, who was talking to her upstairs neighbor.

While Ms. Lyons had her back to us, it was clear she was fidgeting. She twirled her finger around her ponytail. She threw her head back in exaggerated laughter.

"What's the deal with Ms. Lyons and Mr. Stapleton?" I asked Bryant because I'd seen that kind of behavior recently.

"Excellent question!" Shelby exclaimed, which, yeah, felt pretty good. Man, I was really on a roll today. Maybe I didn't need Shelby after all. (Okay, I did. We all knew that.)

"They're pretty close," Bryant stated. "She waters his plants, gets his mail and stuff while he's away."

Shelby narrowed her eyes. "And what is their individual personal status?"

"Huh?" Bryant asked.

"We know Ms. Lyons is divorced, but what about Stapleton?" I clarified. "Is he dating anybody? Does she, you know, like him?"

I shuddered a bit. Not because I cared if Ms. Lyons and Mr. Stapleton got together, but this was hitting a little too close to home with my mom possibly having a secret new boyfriend.

Bryant shrugged his shoulders. "I don't know. Maybe?"

"Interesting," Shelby stated again.

I had no idea why that would be interesting. I mean

grown-ups dated and stuff. It wouldn't mean that they were haunting a building.

Right?

Mr. Barrymore exited the building and approached us. "Mr. Mortimer's fine. Everybody else doing okay?"

Bryant nodded while Ms. Lyons finished her conversation. Hmm, her cheeks did seem a bit more flushed. But again, if adult dating caused hauntings, 221 Baker Street could be next.

Ugh.

"There she is!" Ms. Lyons said as Kaitlin dragged her feet back to us.

She held up a white envelope in the air. "I was hanging on the corner, and a girl asked me to give you this note, Mr. Barrymore."

Shelby approached the envelope now in Mr. Barrymore's hand with interest. "Please."

He opened it up, and all of us leaned in. When he unfolded the piece of paper inside, his eyes got wide. His hands began shaking, and that's when Shelby took it from him.

I looked over her shoulder and nearly gasped. There were letters cut out from a newspaper on pink paper.

"Quite curious," Shelby remarked, and she began examining the note with great focus. "The person who sent this had money."

"What?" Mr. Barrymore said, his jaw practically on the floor.

"The letters were taken from a financial newspaper, most likely the *Financial Times*. It has the salmon-pink print favored by financial newspapers. It all started in the UK in the early 1890s when the *Financial Times* wanted to—"

"Shelby," I said. I didn't think anybody here was interested in a history lesson right now. "But how do you know they have money? Anybody could've bought that paper."

She handed me the letter. "You tell me."

Oh man. She was letting me deduce something again. This meant Shelby trusted me and knew that I was doing better. Maybe the talk I had with her about being nice and friends helping friends really did rub off on her!

I took the letter from her and felt the weight of the paper in my hand. "This is heavy stock paper. Expensive."

"Exactly. What else can you tell me?"

I got that rush I always had when I worked with Shelby. It almost made me forget about how freaked out I was. Almost.

I studied each letter. It was then that I noticed it. All the letters were cut in very clean lines. Usually if someone cut something with scissors you would see where they had to lift the scissor handles again. There's usually a slight mark left behind. This had none. "They used an X-ACTO knife to cut it."

"Good job!" Shelby said, and I felt pretty good about myself. "That is not something people generally have lying around their house. Usually it's used by artists, architects, scrapbookers, et cetera. Or found at a school."

Where was Shelby going with this?

She turned toward Kaitlin. "Can you describe the person who left this?"

Kaitlin tilted her head as she studied Shelby. "I guess. I mean, she was a girl with red, curly hair. Kind of like you. She gave me her name."

The corner of Shelby's mouth turned up. "She did?"

"Yeah, she said it like twelve times to make sure I'd remember it. I mean . . ." Kaitlin rolled her eyes and then went back to her phone.

"Would you care to share this piece of information?" Shelby said, while I held my breath.

"Shelby. Her name was Shelby Holmes."

CHAPTER 11

WHAT?!?!

Every head turned to look at Shelby, while Shelby did something I rarely saw her do.

The great Shelby Holmes burst into laughter. Like real, hilarious laughter. Because this was . . . funny?

"What?" Kaitlin asked. "Do you know Shelby Holmes?"

Yeah, okay. So Kaitlin was the worst witness. She didn't remember our names when she was introduced to us only a half hour ago.

"Honey, that's Shelby Holmes," Ms. Lyons clarified as she pointed to Shelby.

"I don't get it," Kaitlin remarked before looking back down at her phone.

"Oh, how utterly delightful!" Shelby exclaimed with a huge smile on her face. "It seems we have a very worthy foe."

Okay, so this was way worse than I thought.

WAY WORSE.

Shelby thought this was all DELIGHTFUL? Because I had other words I'd use. Like dreadful. Confusing. Scary.

"How can you laugh at any of this?" Ms. Lyons scolded Shelby.

Shelby replied by laughing even harder.

Great.

"Have you heard about this?" Bryant asked as he handed Ms. Lyons the *New York Times* article about Hugo Baskerville's murder.

Ms. Lyons looked panicked as she read about the apartment unit across the hall from her. "I remember hearing that someone had died in the building decades ago, but I didn't know there was a murder! And on my floor!"

"It's true," Kaitlin spoke as she held out her phone. "I googled it. There are a bunch of articles about it. It's even featured on a blog about haunted Harlem."

Shelby scoffed. "Well, yes, because if it's on the internet, it must be true."

I looked at Kaitlin's phone and saw the search results all mentioned Hugo Baskerville's murder and reported ghost sightings. An image search came back with a few sketches of a really big scary dog.

Shelby leaned in close to me and whispered, "Watson, remember that at one moment in time, the internet said we were up-and-coming pairs figure skaters."

Fair enough. Shelby knew how to manipulate the internet, so others had to have the ability to add stories about Hugo Baskerville.

Man, I hoped this was all fake.

Oh, yeah, but let's not forget the most important question: Why would someone go through all this trouble to make it seem like a building was haunted?

None of this made sense. None. Of. It.

Yeah, Kaitlin wanted to move to Brooklyn, but she didn't seem like the kind of person to pull off something like this. It would require looking up from your phone for more than two seconds.

Or maybe that was all part of her ruse?

Who knew? Certainly not me.

"Mr. Barrymore, why would your tenants—many who have lived in the building long before you arrived—not be aware of this so-called haunted building they live in, especially one that's allegedly so well known?" Shelby asked with a raised eyebrow.

"I—I—" Mr. Barrymore stuttered. He hung his head. "I think my uncle knew that if people were aware of the haunted history they wouldn't want to live here. It's not exactly something you'd advertise: close to the subway, eat-in kitchen, and occasional ghost sightings. None of it had been real before this weekend."

"It's not real," Shelby stated flatly. "If the fake claw marks weren't enough, that letter in your hand makes it quite clear something other than the paranormal is at play here."

Shelby had a point. Someone handed Kaitlin that note to give to Mr. Barrymore. It wasn't a ghost.

It was a person. What made that possibly more frightening than a ghost was that person knew about Shelby.

So yeah, this case could get worse.

Cool. Cool. Cool.

Unless Kaitlin was lying and she threw together that note in the few minutes she was gone. As I studied the note, I noticed that each letter was glued on. Kaitlin didn't have enough time to put something so precise together.

So maybe it wasn't Kaitlin?

"But who would do this?" Mr. Barrymore asked.

I looked around at Bryant's neighbors. If Shelby was right, one of them was responsible. Yeah, there was Kaitlin, but what about Ms. Lyons? Mr. Mortimer? The mysteriously absent Mr. Stapleton? I guess even Mr. Barrymore had to be a suspect.

"That's what Watson and I are going to figure out," Shelby said with a flip of her hair as she began to walk away.

"Ah, I guess we're heading out. Bryant, I'll talk to you later." I gave him a nudge on the shoulder. "It's going to be okay, I promise."

Bryant nodded at me, but he didn't look convinced. Couldn't blame him.

I didn't want to make a promise to anybody, especially a friend, that I couldn't keep, but if Shelby said it was nothing, it had to be nothing.

At least I hoped.

CHAPTER

12

"Where are we going?" I asked Shelby as we got on the subway to head downtown.

"To where all good detectives are raised."

Yeah, so that answered nothing.

She closed her eyes and leaned her head back. I knew that meant she was trying to figure this case out.

Shelby wasn't the only one. Okay, I needed to look at the motivation of each of the tenants, if, like Shelby believed, one of them was indeed responsible for faking this haunting.

Kaitlin wanted to move to Brooklyn.

Ms. Lyons had a crush on Mr. Stapleton. Not sure if that was relevant, but Shelby always said to never disregard even the tiniest fact.

Mr. Stapleton was nowhere to be found. He'd also already converted one unit to make his apartment bigger. Maybe he wanted the whole place to himself?

Mr. Barrymore inherited a building that he might not have wanted.

Mr. Mortimer was a tough one. He didn't like the noise coming from upstairs. Maybe he wanted fewer neighbors? He was watching one of those forensic shows, so maybe he'd learned a thing or two.

But how could you fake a haunting when there's an article from a hundred years ago stating that Hugo Baskerville was murdered? The building was even featured on a tour of haunted buildings in Harlem.

I was stumped. I pulled out that old *New York Times* article and read it again. "Hey, Shelby, something doesn't sit right with me with this article."

She opened her eyes. "Why would you say that?"

"You know how in history Ms. Baumstein told us to either read or watch the news ten minutes a day?"

"I'm aware of that requirement. Continue."

"So I've been reading the front page of my mom's *New York Times*. I mean, it's pretty scary, everything going on in the world."

"That's what happens when you put adults in charge," Shelby said.

"Yeah, and well, that article read differently than the ones in the *New York Times*. I get that the article is like a hundred years old, but it asked the question: Did one of the tenants snap? Articles are supposed to report facts, not ask the reader questions. It's more like a gossip site."

"I didn't study the article, as I assumed it was fake." Shelby took the article and glanced at it for about four seconds before handing it back to me. "You make a good point. In addition, if you've ever read any of the pieces the *Times* printed in the early nineteen hundreds the rest would be rather obvious."

I replied by staring blankly at Shelby. Yeah, because I read one-hundred-year-old articles for fun. Come. *On.*

Shelby sighed. "This article was allegedly published in 1919. First, the *New York Times* did not regularly publish bylines for their reporters until later. Second, it refers to the Harlem Renaissance, a term that wasn't coined until 1925 by Alain Locke. Additionally, there were two words in this article that didn't exist back in 1919. *Trendsetter* first was used in 1960, while *scam* first appeared in 1963. *Scam*'s origin is perhaps related to the nineteenth-century British word *scamp.*"

I mean, *really.* Who would know that besides Shelby Holmes?

Seriously, how does she do it? I was exhausted just listening to her. But it did make me realize I needed to study more about my new neighborhood. The rest, well . . .

"It's clear the person pulling the strings is clever, but not clever enough to study etymology."

"Eta-what?"

"The study of word origins and how their meanings have changed through the years."

"Yeah, okay, sure," I agreed with her because I didn't understand how word origins were going to solve this case.

"So if we agree the article is fake, shouldn't we tell Bryant?"

"As you may recall, I'd already referred to it as a sham article in front of Bryant, but we shouldn't divulge our findings." Shelby gave me a pointed look. "All the tenants are suspects, including Bryant and his mother."

"But they're our clients!" I protested.

Shelby scowled. "Don't you think Bryant would just love to have a case that tripped me up? Not as if he had the ability to make that happen."

I hung my head. "Okay, so can we not share *that* with Bryant?"

Here I thought that maybe this case would bring them closer together.

Nope.

"It's important we don't share much with Bryant or any of the other tenants. One of them did this, and I don't want them to know how close we are to figuring it all out."

"We're close?" I asked. I hoped that meant I never had to hear that beast again.

Shelby smirked. "Yes. We're definitely getting somewhere."

The subway pulled into the Times Square station, and

Shelby had us exit. Once we got aboveground, I stopped in my tracks. There were so many people and lights in Times Square, I always got overwhelmed.

"Let's move along," Shelby stated as she began to weave between the tourists and costumed characters on 42nd Street.

I was following her when I felt the buzz of my cell phone in my pocket. I picked it up and smiled when I saw who the text was from.

"Who's the girl?" Shelby asked pointedly.

How did she—you know what? Why did I even ask? Although I'd seen pretty clearly with Ms. Lyons and my mom (*groan*) how body language could show feelings.

"Aisha," I replied. "She's asking about my Halloween plans."

Shelby's face scrunched up. "Aisha from the figure skating rink? Why on earth are you still in communications with her? We solved that case."

"We're friends."

"You like her?"

"I mean, yeah. She's cool."

And pretty and had these big brown eyes and was an amazing skater and I could go on for days.

Shelby stuck her tongue out in disgust. "Okay, Romeo."

"It's not like that," I replied unconvincingly.

"How many friends are necessary?" Shelby asked, then

growled—actually growled—at a family of tourists blocking the sidewalk in front of Bryant Park.

"I like having friends," I stated.

"Yes, but how many does one require? Is there some sort of qualifier on the ideal number of close friends or acquaintances?"

I often had to remind myself that friendship was a very foreign concept to Shelby, but it wasn't something that could be broken down in terms of statistics.

"It depends," I admitted. "I meet people. I get to know them. It sort of comes naturally."

Shelby nodded. "Watson, would it be okay if I only have you as a friend?"

Aw man. That was such a nice thing coming from Shelby.

Before I could reply, she added, "Because I find the concept of having multiple people like you in my life extremely exhausting."

So yeah. Maybe not really a compliment.

When Shelby stopped, I finally looked up to see one of the stone lions that flanked the New York Public Library's main building staring back at me.

"The library?"

"Yes. As I said, it's where all good detectives are raised."

CHAPTER

13

I FOLLOWED SHELBY UP THE STEPS TO THE MAIN LIBRARY entrance. There were people sitting on the stairs hanging out, drinking coffee, or taking pictures of the iconic building.

"Hey, Shelby!" one of the guards greeted us as we walked through the front door.

"Salutations, Frank," Shelby replied.

"Well, hello, Miss Shelby," a woman in a head scarf said as Shelby handed over her backpack for inspection.

"Fatima," Shelby said with a nod of her head.

Was there anybody here Shelby didn't know?

(Probably not.)

We started walking down a long corridor.

"You're going to look at the archives for the *New York Times* to see what we can find out about Hugo Baskerville," Shelby stated. "You'll use microfilm as it can't be hacked."

"Okay," I replied like I had any idea what she was talking about. "What are you going to do?"

"I need to do some research on real estate and gentrification in Harlem." After I stared blankly back at Shelby she clarified, "Gentrification is when an area is transformed to appeal to a high-income bracket. Basically, what's happening to Harlem with all the condos going up and white people taking over what was once a predominantly African American neighborhood."

This time my stare back at her was blunt. I mean, *really*? So I didn't know the word *gentrification*, but I certainly was more impacted by it than Shelby.

Shelby held her hands up. "My parents have been in Harlem for nearly two decades. But your point is taken, Watson. I don't enjoy all the new buildings being built around us. It diminishes the character of the neighborhood."

We arrived at a small room lined with black file cabinets and a cluster of computers in the center.

"Hello, Shelby!" an older white woman with short salt-and-pepper hair greeted her with a smile. "What can I do for you today?"

Shelby handed me a form to sign in.

"My colleague John Watson requires the *New York Times* archives. He'll need your assistance as he's a microfilm novice."

The librarian smiled warmly at me. "Not a problem at all. Why don't you find out the dates you need, and we'll go from there?"

"Ah, Shelby," I stated as I stared at the form. There was one item I couldn't fill out. "I don't have a library card."

"You what? Unacceptable, Watson!" Shelby snapped.

So look, I had disappointed Shelby many times. Mostly because I didn't seem to know some random fact, but this glare she was giving me now. Oh boy. I'd certainly done it.

I couldn't really blame her. I'd been meaning to get a library card since we arrived.

"Aren't writers also supposed to be readers?" she fired at me.

"Yes, and I do read, but I've been using the school library," I defended myself.

"Ms. Shimick, it looks like we'll also need a form so Watson may procure a library card."

The librarian handed me a form, which I put in my back pocket so I'd be sure to have Mom sign it tonight.

Shelby and I sat down at a computer and typed in Hugo Baskerville's name in a database, and a few dates appeared. Shelby wrote them down. I felt a twinge of panic that November 2, 1919, was one of the dates he'd been mentioned in the *New York Times*.

So maybe that article wasn't so fake after all.

We walked over to the line of cabinets that listed dates as far back as 1851. Wow. There was so much history in these cabinets. Shelby opened one up, and it was filled with white-and-red boxes with dates written on them. Shelby grabbed two and handed them to the librarian, who moved us to one of the computers.

Shelby gave me a flash drive. "Ms. Shimick will take it from here. I'll be up on the third floor to work with

the online databases. Save anything you find on Hugo Baskerville on the drive."

Shelby started to turn around, but then said, "Good luck, Watson."

"Thanks." Although why did I need luck? Research was pretty straightforward.

Then the librarian started to unspool a roll of film into the computer. "This one roll has a week of *New York Times* articles. You need to navigate this dial to find what you're looking for."

Yikes. Looked like I was going to need more than luck. I was going to need hours.

My eyes were glazed over, but I did it.

At least I think I did. I saved seven articles about Hugo Baskerville's real estate developments and his obituary. I looked at the entire November 2, 1919, paper, and the only article about Baskerville was the obituary. That article we were given by the tour guide didn't exist.

I was right! That article was fake!

What that meant, I wasn't so certain. But it did seem that the haunting was all a ruse. (Oh please, oh please be true.)

"How are you getting on?" Shelby asked as she walked in with a big stack of papers.

"Good." I held up the flash drive. "No mention of hauntings."

"Yes, because the *New York Times* is a legitimate news source that doesn't give credence to flights of fancy."

"Also, it said in his obituary that Hugo Baskerville died from a fall in his apartment. He wasn't murdered. There was no hound. What did you find?"

"Quite a lot, but there's still more to do."

We got up to exit the library. My eyes were tired, but even though that article was fake, there was something weird happening in the building. And well, maybe there was something we could do to rule out the ghostly.

"Hey, Shelby, when we get back home, I think we need to do my kind of research."

~CHAPTER~
14

THIS WAS PROBABLY A BAD IDEA.

"So you expect me to stare mindlessly at this screen?" Shelby asked as we sat down at her desk after we arrived back at 221 Baker Street.

"You've watched TV before," I stated, even though it was more of a question.

I thought maybe it wouldn't be that bad of an idea to watch one of those ghost-hunting shows, just in case. Besides, we could learn something.

Yes, even Shelby Holmes could still be taught a thing or two. She kept declaring that we were close, but since she wasn't sharing what her theory was, I was going to make her watch this show.

Shelby leaned back on her chair. "On occasion, it's been forced on us at school. Although I do recall watching a delightful educational program as a young child, perhaps around two years of age."

What? Who remembered being two?

Scratch that: Who besides Shelby Holmes remembered being two?

"Yes," Shelby said as she pulled out some Twizzlers hidden in a book. "It was full of colors and puppets. I remember a sizable yellow bird."

"Big Bird!" I replied, with my hand out. Not like Shelby would ever high-five me, but it was nice to know that she watched *Sesame Street* like every other kid.

"Yes, as I said, the bird was sizable." She sniffed.

"No, that's his name."

"Whose name?"

Never mind.

Why did I even bother sometimes?

I typed on Shelby's computer and found a ghost-hunting show Dad and I would sometimes watch. I scrolled through the episodes and found one that took place in a haunted apartment building in New Orleans. I figured that was as close as we were going to get to what we were up against.

I clicked on play and got my notebook out. Hopefully the show would have information that could help us.

On the screen, a trio of white guys interviewed people who'd had haunted experiences in the apartment building. They mentioned a lot of the same things going on in Bryant's apartment: unexplained noises, weird feelings.

My heart began racing as I recalled everything I heard and felt last night.

So what did these dudes decide to do after hearing all those stories? They were going to lock themselves into the building at night. Alone.

These guys were crazy! No way would I ever do that. EVER.

On-screen, one guy held a gadget that could capture spirits' images.

"They had a scientist build that specifically for them," I explained to Shelby. "Isn't that cool?"

"I'm going to set it to a maximum scientific level," the main guy said.

Shelby snorted. "I could acquire something similar at one of the electronic stores near Times Square."

The gadget lit up.

"See!" I pointed to the screen. "Proof there's a ghost. Scientific proof."

"Watson, that gadget is most likely rigged. We're supposed to simply take the word of these gentlemen—and I use that term loosely—whose livelihoods depend on this charade? I think not."

"Well, I take your word a lot of the time that you're correct."

Oops. Did I say that aloud? Well, it was true. I mean, she usually proved herself right. Okay, always. But sometimes I didn't ask her to explain and simply went along with the fact that what was said was correct.

It was a little thing called faith.

Shelby grimaced. "*I* am interested in facts, not ratings."

Okay, she had a point. What a shock.

"Let's watch and see if there's something that could help us." I didn't want to argue with her anymore. Yeah, I knew she wouldn't like this program, but maybe it would give her some ideas. "You got to admit, these guys are kind of like detectives."

"I find that comparison extremely offensive," Shelby said with a huff.

I crossed my arms as we settled into watching them explore the house at night. There were two guys, one a cameraman and the other the lead guy. The third was outside watching all the cameras that they had set up throughout the apartment.

"I've got a bad feeling—my hand is cold," the main guy said as he held out his hand. I also felt cold last night, even though the heat was on. "It's like it's been put in a freezer. 'Are you here? Talk to me!'" he called out.

There was a weird knocking sound.

Both guys started talking loudly. "What was that?"

"Dude, did you hear that?"

"Dude! That was freaky."

"Do these 'dudes' have proper names?" Shelby asked with a tsk. "Additionally, they are talking over themselves instead of listening. Isn't that the point of this farce: to observe, not to make a disturbance?"

"But what could've caused that knocking noise?" I argued.

"It was off camera. It could've been anybody." Shelby paused. "Let me clarify: it could've been anybody with a pulse."

The program cut to another guy who was sitting in a room alone, the night vision camera close to his face. "Are you in here, dude?"

Shelby sighed annoyingly. "The ghosts they are claiming inhabit this apartment are from a time before *dude* was a known slang term. They might as well be saying, 'are you in here, Cyclops?'"

We watched as the guy stared into the camera some more, breathing heavily. Then a lamp in the background fell over. I jumped a bit.

"See!" I said as the guy started screaming and ran out of the room. The program then replayed the incident in slow motion. You couldn't see anything or anybody moving it.

Yeah, so watching this was a bad idea. I was even more anxious now.

"Watson," Shelby stated calmly. "There could've been somebody behind the couch to knock it over. There conveniently was an obstructed view of the lamp."

Okay, she had a point. Again. But still . . . All these shows couldn't exist if they were all fake.

We watched the rest in silence. As the credits rolled, Shelby stood up and stretched. "Well, that program failed in both its attempts at being informative and entertaining."

It was successful in making me more wary of ghosts.

Yay.

I gathered my backpack to head downstairs.

"I'm going to need the evening to think, Watson. We'll return tomorrow after school and stay until we have some answers. These strange occurrences usually happen in the evening. I'm quite looking forward to experiencing them firsthand."

I wasn't looking forward to even walking back into the building. "You might think differently once you're there."

"Oh, I have no doubt it is quite the spectacle." A smile spread on her face. "We have a rather admirable person we're up against."

That was what I was afraid of.

⌐·CHAPTER·⌐
15

WHEN I WALKED INTO OUR APARTMENT, MOM WAS AT THE kitchen counter cutting up some vegetables.

She gave me a kiss on the forehead. "How was last night?"

"It was good," I lied.

She looked at me and placed the back of her hand on my forehead. "You don't seem well. Are you feeling okay?"

You mean besides the fact that we were dealing with something or someone scary and unpredictable? And that I just watched a TV show that had put me more on edge?

That would not go over well with Mom.

"Yeah, just a little tired."

She considered me for a moment. "This is exactly why I don't like school night sleepovers. Sleep is important." (SEE! She does say it!)

I put my stuff down on the kitchen table. "What did you do last night?"

She turned her back on me to get a pan. "Nothing much."

There was a bit of a pause when she said that. Huh. She wasn't telling me the truth.

Okay, okay, yeah, I knew I wasn't being entirely truthful with her, either.

I did a quick scan of the apartment. I saw two wine glasses on the drying rack. Why would Mom need two wine glasses?

"Did you have someone over last night?" I asked.

She stopped cutting the zucchini. She glanced quickly at me. "Why do you ask?"

AHA! That was not an answer! She did the classic answer a question with a question to avoid answering. Yeah, the John Watson of a few months ago wouldn't have thought anything of that.

But now I knew better.

I pointed at the drying rack. "There are two wine glasses."

She froze for a moment. "Look at my detective son. I was so tired from work last night that I poured myself a glass of wine, but forgot and poured myself another one. Your mother is becoming forgetful!"

I studied her. Something was off. I looked closer at the

living room area. It had the same couch and armchair. There was a blanket draped over the side of the couch, but that could be because it was getting cooler.

Then I saw it. Next to Mom's book club book on the coffee table were two coasters.

You didn't need two coasters for one person drinking one glass of wine.

Mom wasn't being entirely forthcoming. Which was a nice way to say that she was flat-out lying.

Here's the thing: Mom would've been open if she had a friend over. That was no big deal. I'd met a few of her work friends. Her book group came over here a couple weeks ago. She'd even stayed late at work a few times to have dinner with a friend.

There was only one reason she wouldn't tell me about having someone over.

My suspicions from yesterday were slowly confirmed.

"Do you believe in ghosts?" I asked her.

"What?" Mom seemed both relieved that I was changing the subject, yet confused about what I was asking. "Is this about those scary movies you and your father have been watching? What did I tell you about that? No more horror movies if you're having nightmares."

"No, it's not that. There's some crazy stuff that happened last night at Bryant's."

I told Mom everything. Every. Single. Detail. At one point, she stopped trying to get dinner ready and sat down.

"So yeah," I finished. "I wanted you to know because we said no more lies or secrets between us."

The look on Mom's face told me what her reaction would be if she did, in fact, see a ghost.

Well, it was official: Mom was dating someone.

CHAPTER
16

"EVERYTHING OKAY, JOHN?"

Dad looked at me with concern as we video chatted after dinner.

"Yeah," I lied. "Just a really long day." Which was entirely true.

Things weren't okay. In fact, everything was the opposite of okay. This confusing case that was giving me a serious case of the creeps. Mom was lying to me about something. My dad was a thousand miles away.

So yeah, not good at all.

"Come on, I know you better than that," Dad said with a tilt of his head. "You can always talk to me."

But could I? That was the worst part of the divorce. I didn't feel like I could talk to either of my parents about the other one. They wanted to live separate lives, and I was the one caught in the middle.

Talk about life not being fair.

"I really miss you," I stated, because it was the truth. Dad's recent visit made me miss him even more now. Before, there weren't memories of him everywhere. Now when I saw Sal's pizzeria, I thought about getting a slice with him. When the Knicks were on TV, it brought back memories of us going to a game at Madison Square Garden. Even walking into the Holmeses' apartment reminded me of how he had to leave abruptly.

He was everywhere, even though he wasn't.

"I miss you, too." He touched the screen. "And listen, I don't want you to get your hopes up, but there's a really good chance I'll be moving to the East Coast at the beginning of the year."

"Really?" I didn't want to think much about it because I *did* have my hopes up.

"Of course. You know I miss my little man. You're growing so much and having all these experiences and your pops is missing out."

I beamed. Maybe things weren't going to be that bad after all.

"How's your mom?" Dad asked.

Then it all came crashing down.

So was I supposed to tell him that Mom was most likely dating? Oh no, was Dad also dating?

You know what, there were certain things a kid didn't

need to know about their parents, and their romantic lives should be one of them.

Yuck.

The truth was having them both move on meant that the fantasy I'd had of them getting back together was just that: made up. Yeah, they were divorced and all and living in separate states, but there was still a part of me that hoped they would eventually get back together and my life could return to normal.

"Mom's good," I finally replied. "Ah, so there's a new case."

I had become a master at changing the subject when it came to my parents. I told Dad all about what was going on at Bryant's apartment building. Well, at least what I knew. Even recounting to him all we've learned and even more we didn't know, I realized that there just might be a case out there that even Shelby Holmes couldn't crack.

Especially since John Watson was absolutely clueless. And confused. And scared.

But I didn't want Dad to know that.

"You be careful," Dad said with a wag of his finger. "I don't like the sound of any of this. So I take it you want to skip *The Haunting of Manor Inn* tonight?"

I nodded. "Yeah. That might be for the best."

"We could watch a ghost-hunting show if you think that would help."

"I tried that earlier with Shelby, and it did not go well."

"I can only imagine. That Shelby is something else."

No kidding.

"I'm serious, John," Dad said in a soft voice. "I want you to be careful. I don't believe in ghosts, but that doesn't mean you shouldn't be cautious with whatever is going on over there."

"I promise." I knew Shelby would never put me in a dangerous situation. Well, again. There was that whole passing out and having to be whisked away in an ambulance, but that was, like, weeks ago.

"I trust you. But I have to admit I'd rather you stick with figure skating cases. Although you're probably falling down on your butt a lot less this time around."

We both laughed. Yeah, I had some issues when it came to staying upright whenever I put on figure skates.

Man, I was so glad that case was over. Not like this one wasn't keeping me up at night.

I yearned back to the days of a good old-fashioned dognapping.

Or, I don't know, maybe people could stop committing crimes in the first place.

But what fun would that be?

Oh great. I was sounding more like Shelby.

That was never a good sign.

CHAPTER 17

"THERE'S ONE THING I CAN'T FIGURE OUT," BRYANT SAID THE next day as we walked to his apartment after school.

One thing? He had only *one thing* he couldn't figure out? Because I had, like, a gazillion. And not just about this case. About Mom. About Dad. About everything.

"What would that be?" Shelby asked as she unwrapped one of the four Levain cookies Bryant bought her.

"If there's somebody doing this, how do they know you?"

Good point. Someone knowing Shelby's name should worry us instead of pleasing Shelby.

"It is safe to presume that your building and those coming and going from it are monitored," Shelby replied.

"Okay, let's say that's true."

"It's true," Shelby stated flatly.

"Yeah, but how do they know *you*?" Bryant glared at Shelby.

"Why would someone know about two young detectives

who solve cases? Ones with numerous satisfied clients? Who are well known in this neighborhood? Who were recently featured in the Harlem Observer, not to mention Watson's blog, which is gaining readers daily?"

Wait a second. Shelby told me she didn't read my blog since she'd lived it. Hmm, maybe she did like reading what I had to say about her.

Uh-oh. Sometimes I wasn't very flattering because I *told the truth.*

Shelby continued, "Bryant, you often underestimate my abilities. Granted, I haven't thus far been able to properly put all the pieces in place for you. But I will. I've done it before. I'll do it again. And must I remind you how detrimental it has been for you to underestimate me in any capacity?"

Bryant sulked for the rest of the walk to his place.

Although he had a reasonable question. How did this person foresee that Shelby would get involved—since she wasn't even brought in until yesterday at lunch? How did they know enough to use her name on the very day she showed up?

My online journal about our adventures *had* gained new readers. We were recognized around the neighborhood, but we weren't that famous. There were only a few photos of us online. (Okay, yeah, I googled myself once. Or a few dozen times.)

How did Shelby fit into all of this?

Maybe Shelby was onto something when she said that Bryant would want to see her fail. Not that Bryant was involved, but maybe it was someone from one of her past cases who had a vendetta against her. Maybe someone she'd been rude to.

So, like, *everybody*.

Could it be Belle from the figure skating cipher? Or maybe one of the Lacys from the dognapping case? I'd hate to think Zane could be behind this, but I'd been wrong about him before.

Wait a second. *Shelby* had been wrong before. The whole Mr. Crosby case. She was blinded by her own ego to see that there was someone pulling the strings. She had simply believed that Miss Adler's School for Girls would move heaven and earth to bring her back. *I* was the one who thought that seemed fishy.

And then we'd met Moira Hardy. Aka the only person to outsmart Shelby. Moira almost got away with blackmailing our teacher and being an all-around horrible person. She had even set a trap for us that we fell right into, locking us in a basement. It was bad, and not just because I ended up in an ambulance due to diabetic hypoglycemia.

But eventually, Shelby had provided evidence that Moira hacked into her school headmistress's email. As a result,

Moira had been assigned volunteer work—a pretty small punishment if you asked me. But Moira had money and her family donated a lot of it to the school, so . . . do the math.

I had hoped we were rid of Moira, but this sounded an awful lot like her. Not the whole haunting business, but being one step ahead and taunting us with that note, which had paper from a financial newspaper. Moira's dad worked in finance. Plus, she loved nothing more than to mess with Shelby and make our lives complicated.

"Hey, Shelby," I started cautiously. "You don't think *she* has anything to do with this?"

"Who?" Shelby asked as she licked chocolate from her fingers.

She was going to make me say it. It's like you-know-who from the Harry Potter books. I didn't want to say her name aloud.

Since Shelby wasn't getting my hints, I took a deep breath. "Moira Hardy."

At Moira's name, Shelby perked up. "Oh, that would be fun!" (Again: Shelby did not understand what "fun" meant.) "How did you make that deduction?"

"If Kaitlin is to be believed, the girl who gave her that letter looked like you. So either whoever did this hired a girl to impersonate you . . . or it could be Moira in a wig."

Moira was a little taller than Shelby and had darker skin,

but skin could be lightened with makeup and Kaitlin didn't comment on her height, probably because she was staring down at her phone.

Shelby didn't respond so I continued, "Plus this person knew you and anticipated your arrival. You weren't at Bryant's long enough for someone to see us enter and then go hire someone. So they had to know you were going to show up."

"That is true," Shelby conceded. "However, if this person is as clever as we think, which Moira certainly is, they'd have realized that you were an acquaintance of Bryant's and I'd eventually be called in."

I bristled at that. Whoever it was assumed I wouldn't have been able to figure it out on my own. Yeah, that was true. But still.

Have some faith in Watson, people!

Shelby remained quiet for the rest of the walk to Bryant's, which meant that she was processing what I was saying. I might be right! (As much as it would be nice to be right, I didn't want it to be about Moira. She was TROUBLE.)

But . . . *why*? A detective always needed to figure out *why* someone would do something (send ciphers, kidnap a dog). There was no reason *why* Moira would be involved with Bryant's building. Right?

The biggest problem with Moira Hardy—she didn't really

need a why. Her only motivation seemed to be bringing Shelby down. Seriously. She only wanted to prove that she was smarter than Shelby, which ended up backfiring on her. But there were so many ways to get back at Shelby (like, say, having all sugar banned in NYC). Why Bryant? Why now?

It seemed like a stretch. Even for her.

So that basically left us with everybody in Bryant's apartment building as suspects. My gut told me Kaitlin wasn't behind it. Yeah, she had a motive, but I didn't think she could pull it off. But we all know my gut has been wrong in the past. Let's hope it was off regarding Moira. And Mom.

As much as Shelby said it was an inside job, everybody in the building seemed really upset about what was happening. Were they all really great actors? Who had the most to gain?

So many questions, so few answers.

When we rounded the corner of Bryant's street we knew right away something was wrong. Really, really wrong.

Outside the building was an ambulance and two police cars. The lights were on, and someone was being carried out on a stretcher.

CHAPTER 18

IT WAS MR. MORTIMER.

He was being treated by two EMTs. He had an oxygen mask over his mouth.

This had reached a whole other level.

A really, really bad level.

"He's my neighbor!" Bryant called out to one of the EMTs as we went running over. "What happened?"

They ignored us and loaded Mr. Mortimer into the back of the ambulance. But he held up his hand and gestured toward the medic who was checking his pulse. He pulled down his mask.

"Are you okay, Mr. Mortimer?" Bryant asked, his voice shaking.

His mouth moved for a few beats. Bryant leaned in. Shelby and I gathered around him as well. His skin was ashen, and he looked more gaunt than usual.

"What is it?" Bryant said as he held his hand.

"I—I—I," he stuttered. "I saw . . ."

Oh no.

Just *no.*

"Saw what? WHAT DID YOU SEE?" Bryant asked, his voice near hysterics.

Have to be honest, I was dreading the answer to that question. No way could it be any good.

Here's the thing: every time Shelby dismissed this case and said there was a logical explanation and nothing otherworldly was at play, something like this happened.

Before Mr. Mortimer could answer, the paramedics put the mask back on him and loaded him into the ambulance.

The three of us stood there dumbfounded as the ambulance sped away. Well, Bryant and I looked lost, while Shelby had her eyes closed. Her mouth was moving slightly.

Bryant began to talk, but I held up my hand to silence him.

"She's figuring something out," I whispered to him.

The front door of the building opened. And there, walking beside Ms. Lyons was none other than Detective Lestrade.

Shelby was not going to like this.

Detective Lestrade was with the New York City Police Department. Her relationship with Shelby was, ah, unusual. I mean, if you really thought about it, any nine-year-old's relationship with a detective should be weird. Shelby and Lestrade often butted heads, mostly because Shelby stuck her nose in the detective's business. But a few weeks ago they kind of came to a, well, I wouldn't necessarily call it a truce. After Detective Lestrade helped us out with Moira, there was almost a bit of respect between the two. Granted, a very begrudging respect.

Shelby was still deep in thought, but I knew she'd want to know about this.

"Um, Shelby," I said quietly.

"I am quite aware Lestrade is here," she replied. She kept her eyes closed for a beat more before she opened them to see my confused expression. "Watson, her car is right there and I got a slight whiff of her perfume when the door opened."

I looked over at the unmarked black sedan. It looked pretty generic to me, but it wouldn't surprise me if Shelby had memorized her license plate number.

Detective Lestrade smirked when she saw us standing outside. "Why am I not surprised you're involved in all this, Holmes?"

"Greetings, Detective," Shelby said with her arms folded.

"You know the cops?" Bryant asked me.

I shrugged. He'd know about it if he read my blog. I went to his violin recital the other day, so he kind of owed me. I know he didn't read it because he didn't want anything to do with Shelby, but hey, it was a pretty good read—it had action! Twists and turns! Sugar! Me!—if I do say so myself.

Shelby gave Lestrade and Ms. Lyons a curt nod. "What happened with Mr. Mortimer?"

"I was walking up the stairs to my apartment when I heard a loud bang from Mr. Mortimer's unit," Ms. Lyons said. There were deeper bags under her eyes. It was clear she hadn't been sleeping. According to Bryant, last night was the same as before. The stomping. The tapping. The howling. The sense something was off. "Mr. Mortimer wasn't answering his door so I called for Jay, but he wasn't home. I ran upstairs to grab the spare key Mr. Mortimer had given me. When I went in his unit, he was passed out on the floor. I then called 9-1-1."

"He stated to us that he saw something," Shelby said.

Ms. Lyons ran a shaking hand over her face. "Yes. He kept coming in and out of consciousness. At one point he told me that he saw . . . a figure."

"Did he describe this figure?"

"No."

"Those were his exact words, 'I saw a figure.'"

Ms. Lyons shook her head.

Shelby sighed. "When recounting a witness's testimony, it's important to be precise. What exactly did he say? And please be as specific as possible."

Ms. Lyons wrapped her arms around herself. "He just kept saying that he saw it."

"Are you positive he said *it*, not *him* or *her*?" Shelby inquired.

"He said *it*. *I saw it*," Ms. Lyons replied solemnly. "And I am positive."

That was not good. Not good at all.

Not like it would've been great if he'd seen someone. But it probably meant it was the beast.

Oh, wow. Just wow. That meant the beast was real. Shelby could say what she wanted about the howling and claw marks, but Mortimer saw something. And was now on his way to the hospital.

Shelby glanced at her watch. "You seem to be home earlier than usual, Ms. Lyons."

That was right! Bryant said she usually got home around four, and it was barely three thirty. What was she up to? Was she responsible for Mr. Mortimer's condition?

"I had a dentist appointment and took a half day," Ms. Lyons stated as she rubbed her jaw.

"Oh, I'm in the process of finding a new dentist. Can you recommend yours?" Shelby asked.

Shelby wasn't looking for a dentist. She wanted to confirm her alibi. Although that didn't mean Ms. Lyons couldn't have come home and done something to Mr. Mortimer.

After Ms. Lyons gave Shelby her dentist's information, Shelby looked her up and down. "Any other information you're privy to about the situation?" Shelby quickly glanced at Lestrade.

"Are you referring to this nonsense about ghosts and howling creatures?" Lestrade asked with a snort. It was a very Shelby response. "Holmes, there is no conspiracy here. Mr. Mortimer is an older gentleman. As far as ghosts or howling dogs . . ." She laughed as she shook her head. "They aren't real."

Shelby looked taken aback. "Of course they aren't real. You and I agree on that fact, Detective Lestrade. However, something is afoot here. Mr. Mortimer's sickness is only the most recent in a string of events."

"This happens every Halloween. Spikes in ghost sightings. It makes people paranoid."

"But the letter Barrymore received," Ms. Lyons said to Lestrade. "There's been a threat."

"What threat? You didn't mention this to me."

Ms. Lyons filled Lestrade in on the details of the ghost tour, the weird letter yesterday, and even the fact that Shelby's name was used. Which seemed to amuse her as much as it did Shelby. (Those two were more alike than either would ever admit.) As Ms. Lyons told Lestrade everything, Shelby looked more and more annoyed. She didn't want Lestrade to be involved. She liked to work alone.

I mean, she didn't mind working with me. That much. I think.

With her chin, Shelby gestured down the street, where Barrymore was running toward us.

"That's the owner of the building," Ms. Lyons told Lestrade.

"What—What—" Barrymore bent down to catch his breath. "I got your message. Is Mr. Mortimer okay?"

Shelby stood super close to Barrymore, stared into his face as she told him about Mr. Mortimer. She was barely a foot away. While everybody else would find this behavior odd, I knew that she was keeping eye contact to see what his reaction would be to everything she was telling him.

Barrymore being a suspect didn't sit right with me. He mentioned how much work it'd been since the issues started up. It had to have gotten in the way of his schoolwork. I doubted he wanted to manage a haunted building.

Yep, I said it. *Haunted.* Because it was!

Case in point: Mr. Mortimer was now on the way to the hospital!

Barrymore had the most to lose if people started to move out because of the beast.

The real-life beast, which Mr. Mortimer saw.

How much more proof did we need?

"Is everybody properly caught up?" Shelby said with a yawn after she finished filling in Barrymore.

Barrymore looked like he was going to faint. He leaned against the building. His skin was ashy. "I can't believe Mr. Mortimer got hurt from all of this."

We were all quiet for a few beats. Yeah, it was scary. All I knew was that there was no way I was ever stepping foot into that building again.

"Well," Lestrade said with a sigh like she had better things to do, "why don't we check out this infamous unit?"

Nope. Not that. Anything but that.

Everybody started heading to the front door, while I couldn't get my feet to move.

"Come along, Watson," Shelby said impatiently.

Seriously, this case. I couldn't believe I was actually going to walk into that unit again.

But at least we had police backup.

I reluctantly began to follow everybody up the stairs.

Shelby decided to fill in Lestrade. "I've been able to rule out infrasound."

Lestrade returned that piece of information with a blank stare. (*I know, Lestrade, I know* . . .) Shelby explained the particulars of infrasound.

"Which has led me to believe that perhaps carbon monoxide poisoning is at play," Shelby explained. "The popularity of ghost stories soared during Victorian times, not solely from the rise of the periodical press, but due to lighting being provided predominantly by gas lamps. The carbon monoxide they emitted would sometimes provoke hallucinations. It can also cause chills and the paranoid feelings of being watched. Mr. Mortimer is an older individual, so this would affect him sooner than the rest of the residents. There are gas stoves in the apartments. Therefore, carbon monoxide is a clear and reasonable explanation."

"All the units have carbon monoxide detectors," Barrymore stated. "It's the law."

"It's the most obvious explanation to the residents' paranoia," Shelby replied. "And batteries can go missing."

Lestrade gave her a thoughtful nod. "Perhaps, but this is most likely a prank, plain and simple."

Mr. Barrymore unlocked the door to unit 5.

"Let me go in first," Lestrade said with a nod. She turned the doorknob and then let out a noise of surprise.

"What is it?" Shelby pushed the door open wide.

Okay, so I didn't think things could get worse with this case. But I was wrong.

Oh, how I was wrong.

My mouth was primed for a scream, but I couldn't let anything out. If I thought I was scared before, nothing had prepared me for this.

There—in the middle of the living room floor—was a pool of blood.

CHAPTER 19

"Hello, what's this?" Shelby replied casually.

Yep, there was a pool of blood, yet Shelby was as calm as ever. Although I had to think that secretly she was excited about the prospect of a murder scene.

That was when I noticed that there was also blood splattered on the wall.

Okay, so things could get even more gruesome.

Cool. Cool. Cool.

Shelby began to march over to the bloody pool, but Lestrade held her arm out. "Holmes! You should know better. I can't have you waltzing around and interfering with a crime scene."

Shelby laughed. Like, a legit laugh. (That was it: she'd officially lost it.) "This is not a crime scene, Detective Lestrade. Take a deep breath."

Take a deep breath? Were we supposed to be calm right now? Because there was absolutely nothing remotely okay about what was happening.

Also, why were we still in this apartment with a killer on the loose?

Lestrade looked skeptical, but did take a little sniff. Then a bigger one.

"See?" Shelby said with a grin.

Before Lestrade could reply, Shelby strode over to the pool of blood, knelt down, *stuck out her tongue*, and then . . .

SHE LICKED IT.

Bryant gagged.

Ms. Lyons let out a gasp.

Mr. Barrymore covered his eyes.

While I couldn't . . .

I just couldn't deal with it.

The great Shelby Holmes had just licked blood.

Shelby licked her lip, which was covered in blood. "Oh relax, everybody, it's corn syrup. I'd recognize the smell anywhere."

Wait. *What?!?!*

That meant . . .

It was fake blood.

"What?" Ms. Lyons said through the hands that were covering her face in disgust.

"It's fake blood," I explained to the confused group. Nobody seemed convinced or more at ease. I didn't blame them.

Shelby was an expert at making fake blood. I didn't even want to get into how I know that fact.

As with every element of this case, this new fact caused me to wonder WHY?!?!

It was still DISGUSTING.

Shelby got down on her stomach. Her eyes level with the blood. No, it was corn syrup, but it really did look like blood. She sprang back up and circled the pool. She set her backpack down and pulled out a tape ruler. She started measuring the splatters on the wall, the distance between that and the mass on the floor.

"What on earth are you up to, Holmes?" Lestrade asked.

"I'm using the cast-off splatters to calculate the height of the person who left this clue."

Clue? I guess that mess could be considered a clue. Someone left this here because they wanted us to think that someone—or something—was murdered. If their goal was to freak out the residents (and yours truly): mission accomplished.

Maybe Lestrade was onto something and it was some Halloween prank. So after tomorrow, would it all stop?

Shelby closed her eyes, her lips moving. She was doing math in her head. And with all the measurements she just made, I didn't think it was as simple as one plus one equals two.

She opened her eyes with a smile on her face. "Okay, this person is on the shorter side. By my calculations, they measure at five feet, two inches. Now, we must take into account that said person was most likely not without shoes. So I place their height at anywhere from five feet one to one and a half inches," she stated with a confident nod.

Lestrade starting writing this down in her tiny notebook. She was listening to Shelby! And believing her! Progress.

I started going through all the people in the building. I didn't know everybody's exact heights, but I believe Kaitlin was on the shorter side.

And where was Kaitlin anyway? She usually was home by now, but she was conveniently nowhere to be found.

Scratch what I said before, *this* was real progress.

Shelby got up from the floor and wiped her hands. "Mr. Barrymore, I recommend cleaning this up as soon as possible. Hopefully the red food dye will not stain the wood. Generally basic soap and water is adequate. However if it stains, you should use a three percent mixture of hydrogen peroxide."

Mr. Barrymore looked at Shelby in disbelief. Not sure if it was from her constant random knowledge or what happened in one of the apartment units under his nose.

He rubbed his head. "Detective Lestrade, I don't care what that was, I don't feel comfortable having tenants in this building anymore. Their safety is my top priority."

Shelby replied, "There is nothing to worry about. As Detective Lestrade stated, this is all some childish Halloween prank. One done at a very amateur level, if I may add."

(Mental note: find out ASAP what Shelby had planned for Halloween, since I didn't want to know what kind of prank she could pull if she thought *that* was childish.)

Lestrade put her notebook back in her pocket. "Holmes is right, there is nothing to worry about."

There was a pause between Shelby and Lestrade. I didn't think either would ever imagine a situation in which they were on the same side.

Freaky indeed.

↩ CHAPTER ↪
20

"WHERE ARE YOU GOING?" I ASKED SHELBY AS SHE WALKED past Bryant's apartment after we left upstairs.

"We have somewhere to be," she replied as she continued downstairs.

I wasn't going to argue since I wanted to get as far away from this building as possible. Shelby could say what she wanted about fake blood, but still . . . None of this was adding up.

"Okay, man, I guess, ah . . . ," I started to say to Bryant, who didn't look thrilled to be left alone in his apartment. Couldn't say I blamed him. "We'll be back."

"Bryant can come along. We may need him," Shelby stated.

Whoa.

Bryant was also surprised. "Really?"

"Really," Shelby replied flatly.

Bryant stood a little taller as he followed us out the building.

Maybe, just maybe they could be friends after all.

"Where are we going?" I asked as we made our way to the subway.

"Brooklyn," Shelby stated as she held up her phone. There was a photo of Kaitlin with some guy drinking milkshakes.

So Kaitlin was our lead suspect.

We were getting somewhere.

"The benefit with someone like Kaitlin is that she feels the need to share every single detail of her life," Shelby explained as we got off at the Borough Hall subway stop in Brooklyn. "One look at her social media profiles has led me to several observations. One: she posts a lot of pictures of her boyfriend. Two: she really likes Brooklyn. And three: every Wednesday after school, they go to Brooklyn Farmacy and Soda Fountain."

"Wait a second," I began as my brain put two and two together. "That means she has an alibi for what happened with Mr. Mortimer and the blood."

"Fake blood," Shelby corrected me. "That could've been left anytime. As for Mr. Mortimer, the carbon monoxide would take a while to get into his system."

"I can't believe Kaitlin would do this," Bryant said as he shook his head.

"You do realize that someone in the building is responsible."

"Yeah, but . . ." Bryant's shoulder sank as he realized she was right.

We arrived at a corner store that had Farmacy written in large letters on its windows and awning. It also said Soda Fountain, so I guess they had ice cream, too. Once we entered, I thought it looked like we'd stepped back in time to an old-fashioned ice cream shop: mosaic tiles on the floor, leather stools facing an ice cream counter.

And there, in the very back, Kaitlin was cozied up to the guy in the picture, who I presumed was her boyfriend. He had straight black hair to his shoulders and tanned skin. His arm was draped around Kaitlin, and they were lost in conversation. They didn't see us come in.

"First things first," Shelby stated as she walked over to the counter and examined the menu.

"You want anything?" Bryant offered.

"Nah, man, I'm okay." I didn't know how anybody could have an appetite after seeing that scene that was staged. Plus, I was getting suspicious that we might be here more for the sugar than the suspects.

As I looked at the other customers, I saw giant sundaes and milkshakes everywhere. Shelby turned around with a huge smile on her face, holding a gigantic sundae with two hands. It was as big as her head. Her actual head, not her head like her ego. Because, then that thing would be the size of the Empire State Building.

"Can you believe they asked me if I wanted a half size?" Shelby said with a snort. The sundae included a huge brownie topped with two scoops of ice cream, hot fudge, whipped cream, and even more chocolate. Because that was what Shelby needed in her life.

No lie, that thing could probably feed an entire army or one Shelby Holmes.

Bryant was not far behind Shelby. He had a milkshake in a tall glass topped with whipped cream.

He took a sip. "So good." He handed his glass out to me. "It's peanut butter. You want a sip?"

"No thanks." I was pretty sure I was going to need extra insulin tonight solely from being in this place.

"Oh, right." Bryant looked down at his sugar-filled glass. "Sorry. I could, um . . ."

"It's fine." At this point I was used to people—particularly one redheaded partner—stuffing sweets in their face. I was more of a pizza-and-chips guy anyway.

That didn't mean I wasn't agitated. "Ah, so are we going to talk to Kaitlin?"

Come on, guys! Eyes on the prize!

Shelby nodded. "Now, Bryant, the most important thing

is to pay attention to every detail when we talk to them. You know Kaitlin better than Watson and I do, so if she does something—a small gesture, an unusual tic—make note of it. There is no detail too small when interrogating someone."

"Got it," Bryant said. He gave me a small, genuine smile as we approached Kaitlin and her boyfriend. The two of them were at a large round table that sat six, but were squished so close together there was plenty of room for us to join them.

"Celebrating something?" Shelby said as she sat down next to Kaitlin's boyfriend.

Kaitlin looked up, surprised. "What—? Why are you—? Did my mom send you?" She fiddled with her long auburn hair, a slight blush spread on her cheeks.

"This place looked so delicious on your profile," Shelby remarked as she scooped up a big spoonful of ice cream.

"What's going on, babe?" the guy said as he looked at us, confused. "Do you know these kids?"

"Hey, man, I'm John," Bryant said as he held out his hand. "I live in Kaitlin's building."

"Hey, dude," the boyfriend said with a nod. "I'm Antonio. Kaitlin's been telling me about all that crazy stuff going on."

"Really?" Shelby leaned closer to Antonio. "What exactly has she been saying? I haven't experienced it firsthand yet and can hardly believe such tall tales."

"And you are?" Antonio asked as Shelby moved her chair even closer to him.

"They're friends of Bryant's. And are very nosy," Kaitlin said, narrowing her eyes.

Huh. Paranoid, Kaitlin? She knew we were there to help investigate. Funny she would leave that detail out. Not like Kaitlin was much for details, but maybe that was her cover. She pretended to not remember who we were or that she was really into her phone, but maybe that was what she wanted us to think.

Her phone wasn't out now. She only seemed to have eyes for her boyfriend.

Who lived in Brooklyn.

The things people do for love.

A pang erupted in my stomach as I thought about what Mom would be willing to do for her new boyfriend. Would we move again? Did the guy have kids? Would I have to go from being an only child to having stepsiblings? There was a time I wanted to have a brother or sister, but now . . . I couldn't handle any more changes.

I felt a light kick under the table. Bryant gave me a look. Shelby was in the middle of talking to Kaitlin about Brooklyn, and I'd completely zoned out.

Some partner I was turning out to be in this case. Maybe if I wasn't so distracted by what was or wasn't going on back at home, everything would start making sense.

Or not.

"Pity about Mr. Mortimer," Shelby stated as she looked directly at Kaitlin.

Kaitlin furrowed her brows. "What about Mr. Mortimer?"

"Oh, you don't know?" Shelby said before putting another spoonful of ice cream in her mouth, dragging out the suspense.

Huh. Kaitlin appeared genuinely confused. Maybe she didn't know.

Kaitlin turned her attention to Bryant. "What happened with Mr. Mortimer? Is he okay?"

Bryant looked to Shelby, but she was too busy eating her sundae. "Ah, he's in the hospital," he explained.

"What?" Kaitlin exclaimed as she stood up. "Is that why my mom kept calling me?" She reached into her purse and got out her phone. She rushed out of the ice cream shop with her cell phone in hand.

"So," Shelby began as she rested her chin in her hand. "Where did you two meet?" she asked a very confused Antonio.

"I gotta check on my girl," he said as he got up and joined Kaitlin outside.

Bryant's gaze followed Antonio out the door, and then he looked back at Shelby. "So what do you think?"

"This is clearly a two-person job. And there we have two people," she said as she gestured to Kaitlin and Antonio outside.

"How do you know it's two people?" Bryant asked.

"Watson?" Shelby said to me.

I was thrown, since I hadn't considered the two-person theory, but I had to think about this logically. If there was in fact no ghost, and it was living, breathing human beings doing this, how were they doing it?

"The sounds upstairs were happening too quickly after the lights. So one person would cut the lights while the other person made the noises?" I threw out.

Shelby nodded, and I felt pretty good that I was able to put a few things together.

"But that apartment is empty when the noises are happening," I argued. "And we don't even know if Kaitlin has access to that apartment. We also don't know—"

"Yet," Shelby interrupted me. "There are certain things we don't know *yet*, but we will." She turned to Bryant. "I need a favor from you."

Bryant looked skeptical. "Ah, what favor?"

"I need a copy of your lease."

The lease? Why would she—

Oh. Kaitlin wanted to move. Shelby needed to see what the renter's lease said about leaving. Wish I'd thought of that.

"Okay," Bryant said with a nod. "I'll ask my mom where she keeps it."

"Splendid!" Shelby remarked, patting Bryant on the back.

Bryant looked uneasily at where Shelby touched him, like he wasn't sure if she was genuinely complimenting him or trying to somehow poison him.

I decided to go with the positive here.

Because whether ghosts existed or not, seeing Shelby and Bryant get along was the most fantastical thing happening in New York City today.

Shelby stood up. "It's time we get back to Baskerville Estates. In light of recent events, I'm looking forward to tonight's performance."

I could guarantee she was the only one.

CHAPTER
21

"INTERESTING," SHELBY SAID AS SHE PACED AROUND BRYANT'S apartment an hour later.

Bryant's mom had texted Bryant where to find the lease. My eyes glazed over after one page since it was all boring legal talk: tenant shall do this and landlord required to do that for *thirty pages*.

"What's interesting?" Bryant asked as Shelby took pictures of a few pages with her phone.

Instead of answering him, she stretched out on the couch, opened a one-pound bag of M&M's (yes, this was after she inhaled that giant sundae), and closed her eyes.

"Don't tell me," Bryant said as he looked over at Shelby. "She's thinking."

I tried to figure this case out, too. So we had an apartment building with weird noises, including footsteps and a beast growling (still no explanations for how all of that was coming from an empty apartment). Claw marks appearing on the door where the noise was coming from (we'd deduced those as fake). The feeling of dread and paranoia of the residents (it wasn't infrasound, but possibly carbon monoxide?). Mr. Mortimer was in the hospital (not good and no explanation for that). The note about the curse (same). The ghost tour and legend of Hugo Baskerville (probably fake?). The blood (definitely fake).

Then we had our suspects. I guess we could cross Mr. Mortimer off the list. Kaitlin was for sure in the lead: she had a motive, she'd handed Shelby that letter, she could've been lying about not remembering Shelby's name, she'd told us she'd googled the legend of Hugo Baskerville and confirmed its existence, and she also had the perfect accomplice: her boyfriend.

But how would Kaitlin even know that Shelby would get involved? I guess she could've read about Shelby on my blog.

Yeah, all signs pointed to Kaitlin, but there was also this creeping feeling I had. You know who also fit that height description from the blood incident?

I didn't even want to go there.

It was starting to get dark out, which meant the noises would start soon.

"So now what?" Bryant asked.

I had absolutely no idea.

None.

"Homework?" I suggested as Bryant and I sat down at the kitchen table. As much as my mind raced with the details of this mystery, I still had a bunch of schoolwork to do. If my grades slipped even a little, Mom would ground me or make me stop working with Shelby.

Mom! In all the excitement since Mr. Mortimer was taken away, I'd forgotten to check in with her. I was positive my phone would be filled with a bunch of texts from her, worrying. We had an agreement I had to keep in touch with her.

Nothing. I did have a text from Aisha. A huge grin spread across my face. I showed Bryant the picture Aisha sent me of her in her Wonder Woman costume for Halloween.

"Oh, that's the girl from the figure skating case, right?" Bryant asked.

Shelby snorted from the couch.

I kept my voice low. "Yeah. I'm going to see her on Saturday. After the competition last weekend, she wants to go to Sal's and eat everything on the menu."

"That's cool, man," Bryant said as he closed his book. "I don't think I'm going to be able to get this reading done with everything going on."

"We'll get to the bottom of this," I assured him, and hoped it wasn't a lie.

"I know you will."

And I don't think I was imagining it, but I swear Bryant looked over at Shelby with a little bit of respect.

"And it's nice you and Shelby seem to be getting along," I said in a whisper.

Bryant recoiled slightly. "I mean, it's nice she's helping, but this is just, like, a case thing. It's not like we'd ever be friends or anything."

He opened his book again and started reading, or pretended to. So much for those two calling a truce, but at this point who knew how long this case was going to last. Maybe if it went on longer—which no way did I want that to happen—they might really start warming up to each other.

Hey, crazier things had happened. (See: the unexplained howls of a beast.)

I shot off a quick text to Mom before I started working. Shelby remained quiet on the couch, save for the occasional crunch of chocolate.

A little while later, Bryant's mom came home.

"Hello, John!" she greeted me as she hugged her son. "Did you find the lease?"

"Yeah, thanks," I said.

"Anything new today or do I not want to know?"

We filled her in. With each new piece of information— Mr. Mortimer, Detective Lestrade's involvement, and the fake blood—she became more and more distressed.

"Maybe we should go stay with your aunt for a few days," she suggested.

Couldn't really blame her. As much as Shelby and Lestrade could dismiss this as a prank, they were the ones who had to live here.

"That's not necessary," Shelby replied from the couch.

Bryant's mom yelped in surprise.

"Oh, sorry, Mom," Bryant replied. "Ah, that's—"

"Shelby Holmes!" his mom replied with a smile. "Yes, I know you from John's recitals. You're such an impressive violinist. And, of course, from John's blog."

Okay, the two Johns was confusing (which was precisely why he and I went by Bryant and Watson at school). But Bryant's mom had read my blog!

"Pleasure," Shelby replied from the couch. She kept her eyes closed.

"Would you like to stay for dinner?" Bryant's mom offered as she unpacked her bag of groceries.

Before we could reply, the lights flickered.

Here we go again . . .

"Ah, Shelby," I said.

Shelby's eyes popped open. A smirk on her face as the lights began to flash for a few seconds longer until they went out completely. "Cutting the power is as easy as a simple flip of a switch."

The silence was too much. My nerves were on edge, knowing what was coming next.

Bryant and his mom turned on their flashlights and lit a few candles.

Nothing. It was eerily quiet.

The candles went out right as the footsteps started up.

STOMP.

Whoooosh.

STOMP.

Whoooosh.

STOMP.

Whoooosh.

I held my breath as I waited for the dog to start howling. That was the worst.

The tapping began instead.

Taaaap. Taaaap-tap.

Some of the taps were longer than others.

Tap.

Taaaap.

Shelby jumped up from the couch.

"What is it?" I asked while Bryant and his mom held each other.

"It's Morse code," Shelby replied. "Watson, write these letters down."

I flipped over the notebook from math class and started writing down what Shelby said.

"T. O. U. T."

Tout? That made no sense, but I kept writing the letters as Shelby told me: *G* and then *E* and another *T*, followed by an *O*.

She stopped.

"T. O. U. T. G. E. T. O," I read from my notebook. So basically gibberish. Pure gibberish. It wasn't some code. It was just really unnerving noise. That was this person's goal, to make us uncomfortable.

Once again, point culprit. Or culprits.

"I was late decoding it when it started, but it's repeating itself." Shelby looked at the ceiling. "Oh, I just love it when a perp starts chatting. If you let them talk long enough, they'll eventually give themselves away."

"Talking?" Bryant's mom said. "I don't understand. What are they saying?"

"It's quite simple," Shelby said with a grin.

We all waited for her to finally fill us in.

"Get out."

ᴄ·CHAPTER·ᴏ
22

Nᴏʙᴏᴅʏ ɴᴇᴇᴅᴇᴅ ᴛᴏ ʙᴇ ᴛᴏʟᴅ ᴛᴡɪᴄᴇ.

Bryant's mom rushed into her bedroom while instructing Bryant to pack his bags. Someone knocked on the door, and Ms. Lyons came in to ask what was going on. As soon as Bryant told her what the tapping meant, she ran back up to her apartment.

"Ah, maybe we shouldn't panic," I said, even though *I* was panicking. I'd be doing the exact same thing if this happened back at 221 Baker Street.

And I'm not going to lie: I wanted to get out of there as quickly as possible. Because if the culprit was willing to go to such lengths to frighten people—even land Mr. Mortimer in the hospital—who knew what they'd do next?

Shelby, however, stood back and watched. She didn't say a word. I knew she was looking for clues in the behavior of the neighbors.

Mr. Barrymore appeared at the apartment door. "I'm going to check in upstairs."

Shelby approached him. "I'd love to join you!"

He gave her a weird look, because nobody should be that excited to enter a room where creepy noises were coming from.

Shelby pulled a flashlight from her backpack and illuminated it. "Shall we?"

She didn't tell me to follow her, but I knew I had to see the apartment for myself. There was no way the unit would be empty with all that noise. Someone had to be in there. It was the most logical deduction.

"I'm glad to have someone else witness that the apartment is empty," Barrymore stated right as the howling started up.

HOOOOOOOWWWWWL.

We went up a few more stairs.

HOOOOOOOOWWWWWL.

Why were we walking closer to the apartment?

HOOOOOOOOWWWWWL.

I needed to get out of there.

Barrymore paused outside unit 5. "Are you sure you want to do this?" he asked as another howl came and sent a chill down my spine.

"Yes, please," Shelby replied excitedly.

As Barrymore put the key into the lock, the howling stopped. He opened the door and nothing. The apartment was quiet and empty.

Shelby stormed inside and pointed her flashlight beam around the apartment. As she took a few more steps, she bounced a bit on her feet and pointed her flashlight down at the ground.

I took a few cautious steps in and felt that uneasiness again. It wasn't that heaviness like before, but I felt off balance.

Something was seriously wrong with this apartment.

"I think I should check in on everybody," Barrymore said as he gestured for us to follow him out of the unit. I was more than happy to get out of there.

Shelby narrowed her eyes as she took one last look around.

We went back downstairs to Bryant's place.

Barrymore saw the open suitcases. "Where are you going?"

"Jay, we can't possibly stay here another night," Bryant's mom answered. "It's getting to be too much. I'm sure Shelby and Watson will get to the bottom of it, but for now, my son and I need to go somewhere safe. And sleep."

By her haggard and stressed expression, I wasn't sure if sleep was ever going to be possible for her again.

Right then, the lights flickered back on. We all blinked at the brightness.

"I completely understand," Mr. Barrymore conceded. "I'll look at the lease and see if there's any leeway I can give you if you decide to leave. I wouldn't be able to look at myself in the mirror if I held you to your contract at this point."

"I've already examined the lease," Shelby informed him. "As their landlord, you'd be able to waive any fees for early termination."

"Why, I—I—" Mr. Barrymore stuttered. "I hope that won't be necessary. However, my main priority is to ensure my tenants are taken care of. If you'll excuse me." He walked out of Bryant's apartment and went back up to the Lyonses'.

There was another set of footsteps coming up from the first floor. Shelby walked over to the door. "Hello," she said.

"What on earth is going on?" a man's voice came from the hallway.

"It seems your neighbors are quite dramatic," Shelby said with a smirk. "Mr. Stapleton, I presume."

I peeked my head around the corner to see a guy in his late thirties wearing a nice suit, holding a suitcase. So this was the missing upstairs neighbor.

"Yes," he said, surprised. "Wait a minute." He looked between Shelby and me. "I don't believe it! Shelby Holmes and John Watson—cool!"

What? This dude seemed excited we were here.

But hold up. Just hold up. How did he know us? Maybe he was responsible for all of this? He'd been mysteriously "away" all week. He knew who we were—therefore he would've known that I was friends with Bryant. Bryant would ask for my help and I'd bring in Shelby.

He also just happened to pop in right after the lights came back on.

Stapleton also would've had the means to hire someone, based on his tailored suit and shiny, polished leather shoes. His low-fade hair was freshly shaved. And I couldn't be sure, but his nails were really neat like he got a manicure or something. Yeah, this guy clearly had money if he was going to pay for someone to cut his nails.

So he also could've hired someone to do his dirty work.

Mr. Stapleton had two units converted into one. What if that wasn't enough for him? He wanted more space so he hired someone to mess with the neighbors.

Yes! That had to be it!

Mr. Stapleton's face beamed as he continued, "Linda told me that you were here so I looked you up online and read your blog."

Aka doing research on us. Trying to find our weakness.

Stapleton looked around at the chaos of his neighbors. "At first I dismissed all these rumors about a beast howling through the night and ghosts and whatnot. But based on your blog it appears you only take cases with merit. So I guess I am both relieved and nervous that I find you two standing here."

Flattery wasn't going to get him anywhere with us.

Shelby regarded Stapleton cautiously. "Do you speak to Ms. Lyons regularly?"

"We text while I'm away," he replied as he pulled on his cufflink. "She waters my plants."

"So she has a key to your apartment."

"Yes! I guess you could say that Linda is the patron saint of this building. An excellent neighbor. I think she has everybody's keys. We can't always rely on Barrymore being around, especially since he has classes and an internship that keep him busy. His uncle, who was a wonderful man, pretty much never left the building."

This dude was giving us lots of information, but one thing stood out: Ms. Lyons has keys to every apartment. So she had access.

Hmmm. Maybe it was Ms. Lyons in cahoots with Stapleton. She appeared to have a crush on him. Maybe they wanted the building all to themselves!

Or maybe Kaitlin stole the keys from her mother!

Everybody looked super guilty right now.

Stapleton rubbed his hands together. "So what's your theory?"

Yeah, like we were going to tell him. Why was he so curious? Something was up with this guy.

Shelby yawned. "I am not at liberty to discuss until all the facts have presented themselves. Yet with each passing minute, we make new and fascinating discoveries."

Shelby scanned him at that moment. Oh, he was going to be in for it.

Stapleton laughed. "You're even more intriguing in person." He then turned to me and said, "Not that you don't properly capture her spirit in your blog, Watson!"

"Thanks!" I replied with a proud smile, before I had to remind myself that he might be the culprit.

I would not be thrown off by compliments about my writing (even though it was nice to know I was gaining readers).

"Mr. Stapleton, I'm so glad to see you," Mr. Barrymore exclaimed as he came down the stairs. "As you can tell, we have a bit of a situation going on."

Shelby leaned against the wall as Barrymore described recent events.

"Oh no," Mr. Stapleton said. "That's not good."

"Thomas!" Ms. Lyons came down the stairs. She smoothed out her hair as she approached him. "I'm so glad you're here. It's been awful. Be happy you were away."

"Yes, how was London?" Shelby asked.

Mr. Stapleton did a double take at Shelby before breaking out into laughter. "You really are something else."

"And did your meeting with Barclays go well?"

"Extraordinary!" he exclaimed with a laugh.

Because this was funny? I mean, yeah, Shelby's ability to know all this stuff was, ah, extraordinary, but his neighbors were freaking out.

"Thomas." Ms. Lyons put her hand to her forehead. "We've had enough of it. We cannot spend another night here, especially Halloween. Could you even imagine?"

"Well, then, I'll pack another bag and we'll go somewhere safe," Mr. Stapleton said with a nod.

Ms. Lyons's face lit up as Stapleton put his arm around her.

Hmm, she certainly didn't seem upset that she had to abandon her home now.

Maybe Ms. Lyons and her daughter have more in common about their feelings for Baskerville Estates than I originally thought.

Shelby cleared her throat, and everybody looked at her. "Watson and I will prove once and for all that there is no such thing as ghosts and that this building is safe."

We would? But how?

You know what, I didn't really want to know because no way would this be good.

Even if it wasn't ghosts, we were dealing with someone who had gone to great lengths to terrify people.

Shelby crossed her arms. "It was an idea that began to form thanks to something Watson showed me on a so-called television program."

Oh! That *did* help! Maybe we were going to use a cool gadget?

"Yes," Shelby continued. "Watson and I will be spending tomorrow night in this building. Alone."

No.

Seriously? Out of everything we saw *that* was what Shelby got out of it?

This is what I get for having Shelby Holmes watch TV.

Yeah, so not happening.

Just nope. Nope. Nope.

Then it hit me, what tomorrow night was. "You can't mean . . ."

"Yes, Watson, on Halloween."

⌁ CHAPTER ⌁
23

EVEN THOUGH OUR SKILLS WERE IN NO WAY EQUAL, SHELBY and I were considered partners.

So it would've been nice if Shelby consulted me before she declared that we would be spending the night in a haunted apartment building. *On Halloween.*

But why would she start filling me in now?

My mind told me it wasn't haunted. I'd listened to all of Shelby's explanations. But there was a part of me that was a little unsettled by the prospect. We still couldn't account for HOW the noises were coming from an abandoned apartment upstairs or WHO was doing this or WHY. You know, the three most important questions to answer when you're a detective. At this point, I'd just settle for WHO. So everybody could move on, not out.

As much as I didn't want to go over to Bryant's tomorrow night, I knew Shelby wouldn't let anything bad happen to me.

There was a text from Shelby on my phone, **Come upstairs and bring your laptop.**

I closed the math book on my desk and went into the living room, where Mom was typing into her phone. That secretive smile on her face again.

You know what, let me first tackle the mystery of Bryant's apartment before I even deal with what was going on with Mom.

"Mom, I need to go upstairs to Shelby's. Can I borrow the laptop? I need to ask her a question about a school assignment."

"Go right ahead," Mom replied without really looking up from the phone.

I climbed the stairs to 221B. Shelby's mom answered the door. "Well, hello, John! So great to see you."

"Hi, Mrs. Holmes, Shelby wanted me to stop by."

"Hello, John!" Mr. Holmes echoed as he came up to give me a pat on the back. "We are both incredibly grateful for all that you've done for Shelby!"

Um, okay.

They both beamed as they looked at me with their arms around each other.

"Ah, you're welcome," I replied, even though I have no idea what they thought I did. Although unlike their daughter, Mr. and Mrs. Holmes were generous with compliments and basic human decency.

"Shelby's upstairs, no doubt plotting something." They both laughed while I went up to Shelby's bedroom.

"Come on in, Watson," Shelby called out before I could even knock on the door. I opened it up to find . . . Shelby not there. I looked around her messy bedroom. It wasn't like there were many places for her to be.

"Down here," she called.

I got on my knees and saw Shelby lying under her bed.

"Oh, so are you and Michael playing the real version of hide-and-seek?"

"Absolutely not," she replied. She closed her eyes. "A concentrated atmosphere leads to concentrated thought."

Ooookaaaay.

"I take it you're trying to figure out something about this case."

"Yes! There's nothing more stimulating than a case when everything goes against you."

She sounded excited, while I was tired. And wanted to get to the bottom of it.

"Do you think Ms. Lyons would have had a key to the apartment with the noise?" I asked. We already knew she had keys to Stapleton's, Mortimer's, and the Bryants'. Why wouldn't she have ones belonging to the person who had lived in that unit?

"The probability is high. Additionally, there is no law in New York State requiring a landlord to change the locks after a tenant leaves," Shelby stated, her voice a bit muffled from being under the bed.

"So whoever lived in my mom's and my place could just walk in whenever?"

"Very unlikely, Watson. The former tenant of 221A was a serial killer, who is currently on the loose. Why would he go back to his former residence?"

"WHAT?" I screamed as my heart plummeted.

Shelby snickered as she scooted out from under the bed. "Relax, I am only joking."

"WHAT?" I repeated. It wasn't like my nerves weren't already shot. I mean, COME. ON.

Shelby tilted her head at me. "Isn't humor a desirable trait people look for in a friend?"

Seriously? Nothing was ever easy with her.

"But the case is not why I called you up here."

Oh, so the purpose of this visit wasn't a heart attack? Good to know. I mean . . .

"You," she stated.

"Me?"

Great. So I was up here because she was going to criticize me or pick apart something I did or didn't do.

True, I was never going to learn unless she told me if I missed a clue, but still. She was the least patient teacher ever.

Shelby sat on the edge of her bed. "I need your focus to be a hundred percent on every element we come across tomorrow night."

"I'll be focused," I replied. I couldn't imagine not being on edge to every sound or movement at Bryant's place.

"I can't have you distracted about your mother's new beau."

Oh no.

No.

My suspicions were correct.

"I take by the way your face fell right now that you have not received official confirmation from your mother."

"No."

Shelby perked up. "So you only know this by deduction?"

"Yeah."

"Well done, Watson! Tell me how you came to your conclusion."

I told her about the extra wine glass and coaster, how I knew she was lying, and about her facial expressions when she was texting. Yeah, it wasn't a lot, but I got it right.

"Excellent job!" Shelby replied.

Okay, that felt good, but still. Mom had a boyfriend.

"Wait, how do *you* know?"

"Your mother, while a very attractive woman, has been paying more attention to her appearance: hair is kept, slightly more makeup, more accessories and fitted clothing. She also smiles like she has a secret."

Yeah, a very, *very* big secret.

"It's time you had some concrete evidence so you can stop wondering." She held out her hand.

"The laptop?" I gave it to her.

Shelby walked over to her desk. She opened the laptop and began typing immediately. "We can access your mom's text messages."

"Wait!" I called out. Wasn't this crossing some sort of line? Invasion of privacy? Snooping? "Shelby, I don't think this is right."

Shelby lifted her eyebrows at me. "Do you want to know the truth or not?"

Ugh. She had me there.

Okay, so while I knew it was wrong, Mom wasn't being honest. So what else was I supposed to do?

Yeah, that's how I was going to tell myself that spying on Mom was justified.

Don't judge.

I sat down next to Shelby. "Okay, but only tell me the basics." I didn't want to read any mushy texts between my mom and some dude.

Yuck.

Man, I needed a vacation. Between getting no sleep a week ago because of the figure skating cipher and this case and, you know, finding out Mom was dating.

Good thing I was heading to Kentucky in a few weeks for Thanksgiving to see Dad.

Uh-oh. Dad.

So now that I had confirmation, was I supposed to tell him?

No way. I had enough to deal with.

Honestly, that was what hurt the most. Knowing my parents were moving on, while I only wanted things to stay the same. I knew that was impossible with us living so far away, but a boy could dream.

"Okay," Shelby said as she scrolled through messages. "His name is Andre. He's also a doctor. Very intelligent. Writes in complete sentences. No emojis, thank goodness. Same for your mother. It's refreshing when adults behave like adults."

Even though Shelby's back was to me, I could hear the eye roll in her voice.

"He knows about you."

"He does?"

"Of course, Watson. Your mother has great affection for you. He asks about you, but your mother is not ready for you to meet yet, which means things aren't that serious. If it was, she'd tell you. She wants to protect you."

"I'm not ready to meet him," I blurted out.

Shelby turned around. "Then if this comes up, you need to state that. Many obstacles can be eliminated if people decide to be truthful with each other."

Said the girl who just hacked into my mom's text messages.

And didn't talk to me before signing us up to spend Halloween night at a haunted apartment building.

And always waited until the last minute to fill me in when she figured something out.

I should probably take a page from Shelby and be open with her.

"Hey, Shelby, maybe you could be more truthful to me about our cases?"

She appeared genuinely confused. "Whatever do you mean? I've never once lied to you about a case."

"Yeah, but you also don't fill me in on things."

She scoffed. "I tell you information when you need to know it." She then gave me a curt nod to signal that this conversation was over.

That went as well as I thought it would.

Then Shelby gave me an encouraging smile. "So what are you going to do about your mother?"

"I don't know." I didn't want to talk to Mom about it because then it would be real. But it was real.

"Well, you do need to get permission to spend tomorrow night at Bryant's."

That was something else I'd been avoiding. She knew about the case, so I couldn't imagine she'd be thrilled by this prospect. Part of me wanted Shelby to tell me I couldn't do it so I could bail, but I didn't want to leave her alone.

For better or worse, I would come face-to-face with something tomorrow night. Funny, coming face-to-face with a beast wasn't as scary anymore now that I knew Andre wasn't a figment of my imagination.

I had to get Mom to let me spend another school night at Bryant's. I reminded myself that I was doing this for him. Mom would know how important that was for me.

"What did you tell your parents about tomorrow night?" I asked. Shelby had it worse. She was going to have to get her parents to agree to let her spend the night at a boy's, even though Bryant wouldn't be there.

Shelby shook her head. "Once I used the word *friend* in reference to someone besides you, my parents were more than happy to grant my request. They were quite pleased that you apparently seem to be rubbing off on me."

Ah, right. Now their gratitude made sense. They were under the impression that Shelby was making more friends because of me.

Technically not true, but not the worst thing that happened this evening at 221 Baker Street (again: the spying of my mom's texts).

"Although they had a condition." Shelby scrunched her face.

"What was it?"

"They want to meet Bryant and his mom. They insisted upon personally dropping me off after dinner."

"You talked to Bryant?" I asked.

"No." Shelby grimaced. "I need you to see if he and his mother would be up for this silly charade."

"Yeah, no problem." I figured that would be easy enough.

"You can walk over with us if you'd like."

"Sounds good." No way was I going to miss a sure-to-be-super-awkward encounter.

Shelby trying to be someone's friend was a stretch for her acting skills. Her *and* Bryant pretending to be buds, well, that was going to be something else. I was definitely going to have to run interference.

"One more thing," Shelby said as I started heading out the door. "I need to take a closer look at the *New York Times* article."

"They're all on there," I stated, and pointed to the red flash drive that was on her desk.

"No, I need the fake one. I never gave it a proper look."

"Okay." I pulled the wrinkled piece of paper from my backpack. She had looked at it enough to know that some of the words weren't used back when the article was allegedly written. What else was there?

I was getting ready to leave, but then something hit me. In the chaos and confusion in the apartment building it had slipped my mind.

"Hey, Shelby, how did you know that Stapleton was just in London? And for a business meeting?"

"It was quite obvious," she stated flatly.

And there we go. She *was* disappointed in me. What did I miss in the hallway? I mean, I figured out the guy had a manicure. That should've counted for something.

"His luggage tag said LHR, which is the airport code for London's Heathrow airport. As far as his meeting, since we hadn't yet had a chance to make his acquaintance, I did some research online. Like Kaitlin, he posts quite a lot on social media, including about his, and I quote, 'big time meeting.' All this oversharing online is very helpful when working a case."

"So he hadn't even been in the country and couldn't be involved."

"Technically. While Stapleton wasn't physically here, he could be the one pulling the strings. I'm currently working it all out and should have every piece in place shortly. Anything else?"

I shook my head. "See you tomorrow," I said as I headed for her bedroom door.

"Yes, and Watson?"

I turned around. "Yeah."

"Details. It's all in the details."

CHAPTER 24

"How's Shelby?" Mom asked when I arrived back at our apartment.

"She's Shelby," I replied. We both laughed for a beat.

I also had a hard time looking at Mom in the eyes after we, well, Shelby hacked into her texts.

Huh, this must've been what she felt like when I kept the cases from her.

"What is it, John?" Mom asked, concern clearly on her face.

Guess you didn't need to be a detective to figure out I was a bit off. I'd vowed to be open and honest with her so I guess it was now or never.

"You know how things have been a little surreal over at Bryant's?"

Mom nodded.

"Well, it's gotten worse. I feel really bad for him and his mom. We've gotten to know their neighbors, too. We're close to figuring this out, at least according to Shelby. And she sort of bragged that she and I could spend Halloween there and well . . ."

I decided to let Mom fill in the blanks.

She grimaced. "I thought you said you were going up to Shelby's to discuss homework."

It just slipped out. "And I thought you said you were alone the other night. So who's really the one lying?"

Oops.

Mom's eyes got wide. "John Howard Watson!"

Yikes. The whole name was never a good sign.

But she had lied to me.

"I don't think you understand how much I've been dealing with," I said with a stomp of my foot for emphasis.

Mom sat down on the couch. "So why don't you explain it to me?"

Then it came rushing out. All of it. Everything I'd been feeling since we came here.

"First, we had to move to a new city and I was okay with all of that. I've gotten used to moving, but it was without Dad. So, new home, new life without my father. I can't really talk to him about you because you're the reason we moved in the first place!"

Mom cringed, even though I know the separation was mutual.

"And now this! You're dating some guy, and you don't tell me? How am I supposed to handle one more change, and a big one? Why can't it be like it used to be?" My voice cracked on the last bit because that was the real heart of the problem.

Mom waited for me to continue, but I was done. I didn't have anything more to say. I was tired. I was confused. About the case. About life. About my family. About all of it.

"Come here," Mom said as she patted the spot next to her.

I dragged my feet over and plopped down. She put her arm around me.

"Oh, honey, I know this has been such an adjustment for you. And it's a lot, but you seemed to be adjusting so well."

"I liked my old life."

"I know you did. But don't you like this one?"

I thought about it. I liked New York. I liked my new friends and working with Shelby. But there was something missing, and I shouldn't have to say it.

"I do, but I want my dad to be part of it."

Mom held me closer. "He's trying, John. You have to believe it. We're working on it. You know we don't get much say where we go with the army, but we want to do what's best for you. You'll see your dad more. I promise you that. And I want you to talk to me about it. Promise me you won't hold it in?"

I nodded while I fought back tears. "Okay, but we also promised that there wouldn't be any more lies. I've been honest about this weird case, so it kind of stings that you won't tell me what's going on with . . ." I couldn't even say it. "That I have to deduce what's happening." (And get Shelby's help, but I wasn't about to add that.)

"I'm sorry, I truly am." Mom sighed. "You have to remember I'm new to this whole being-single-and-dating scene. I have met someone. However, it's still new. I didn't tell you because I'm not even sure how I feel. I know how much you miss your father, and I didn't think you were ready to know that I'm moving on with that part of my life."

There it was. The most frightening thing of all. We were all moving on from the life that we'd had.

Mom: dating someone.

Dad: hundreds of miles away.

Me: still getting adjusted to this new life.

"Are you okay?" she asked as she rubbed my cheek.

"I guess."

I really did like my life here. I just miss having a mom and dad together. I know they're both happier now, but that doesn't mean it still doesn't sting.

"I promise I'll tell you when there's something to tell. Unless you want to know all the details—I'm more than happy to share." Mom nudged my shoulder.

Did I really want to know? I mean, my mom and guys? Ewww.

"No thanks," I replied, to which Mom laughed.

"Yeah, I thought so. Although I should know better than to keep anything from my son, the detective." She kissed me on my forehead.

We both sat there for a while. Telling the truth was the best option. Did it hurt to know that Mom was moving on from Dad? Yeah, but deep down I knew this day was going to come.

Plus, this dude might not be around that long. Mom certainly wasn't going to introduce me to anybody who wasn't important to her.

So maybe I had some more time to get used to the idea.

"Now I have a question for you about this case," Mom said.

I was grateful to think about something else. "Okay."

Mom studied me for a second. "Let me make sure I

have this straight: Bryant thinks his apartment building is haunted. There have been all these strange occurrences, and you want to spend Halloween night there with Shelby?"

Yeah, it was a totally bad idea. Why did I think she'd ever go for this?

"Well, I don't think *want* would be the word I'd use," I admitted.

She shook her head with a laugh. "You know I'm a person of science, John. I don't believe in the supernatural. More importantly, I believe in you and Shelby. So you can go, but you have to text me every hour."

No way. She was giving me permission to do it? I didn't know if I should be relieved or worried. Because this meant we were really going to do this.

So yeah, worried.

"Are you sure?" I asked. I know Shelby said never to question somebody after you got the answer you wanted, but I couldn't believe Mom was agreeing to the overnight.

Mom nodded. "I've always felt bad you couldn't experience Halloween like everybody else as a kid. You got to dress up and go around, but you never got to enjoy your candy haul. So I want you to spend Halloween doing something fun."

Fun? Mom thought that spending the night in a possibly haunted apartment building was a fun plan?

Okay, she and I also needed to discuss the meaning of the word *fun*.

"Thanks!" I gave her a kiss good night and headed into my bedroom. I knew I'd need a good night's sleep since I really doubted I'd get any tomorrow night.

There was a text from Shelby on my phone, I'm so sorry, Watson. I should've listened to you.

Ah, *what?* Did Michael get ahold of Shelby's phone, because that was not a text Shelby Holmes would ever send.

What? Is everything okay? I replied because Shelby must've hit her head or something.

I know who else is involved, and we could be in real danger.

CHAPTER 25

Y<small>EAH, SO</small> I <small>GOT ZERO SLEEP.</small>

Because did Shelby fill me in on what I was right about?

Of course she didn't.

"Shelby," I prodded her as we started walking to Bryant's after dinner with her parents. "You've got to fill me in. How are we in danger?"

"Everything will be fine, Watson," she tried to assure me for the four thousandth time that day. "Just a few more details for it to all come together."

"But you said danger!" I said quietly so her parents couldn't hear, as they were a few feet behind us.

"I've got it taken care of."

Yeah, okay, that explains absolutely nothing.

"But, Shelby, remember that whole conversation we had last night about how it would be better for people to be truthful with each other? Maybe you should fill your partner in?"

She snorted. "It's more exciting this way."

"TO WHO?" I croaked out.

COME. ON.

"Okay, okay, at least tell me who your lead suspect is."

Shelby, annoyingly so, returned my question with a question of her own. "Who is yours?"

I shrugged. "I guess Ms. Lyons."

Her having the keys and her relationship with Mr. Stapleton—who could afford to hire help—tipped her to the lead.

"Never guess, Watson." Shelby tsked. "Guessing is for circus con men. Look at the evidence."

That was the problem. We really didn't have any save that one article that proved to be fake and that letter. That was it. Everything else *was* Shelby guessing: that carbon monoxide was responsible for the weird feeling. That the hound noises came from a recording. But we didn't have proof. We didn't know how all of that could come from an empty apartment.

But I did have a feeling in my gut about Ms. Lyons.

"Okay, well, we know most people trust Ms. Lyons with their keys. She would have access. And she lives across the hall so she could've easily gone in and out."

Shelby looked thoughtful. "What would be her motive?"

"Well, Mr. Stapleton has a whole floor to himself, so perhaps she wanted to do what he did. Or it's obvious she likes him, so maybe, I don't know, she wanted to have the building for just the two of them. Or it could be Kaitlin. She could have taken the keys from her mom, and her motive is clear: she wants to move to Brooklyn. This would help her get out of her lease."

Even I could admit I was grabbing at a lot of straws.

Although . . . I didn't know much about renting apartments, but I remember Mom saying that the rules and leases in New York City were strict, so maybe I was onto something. We're lucky to have Mrs. Hudson as our landlady. She's more of a mother hen than an overbearing super.

"That would be a rather logical deduction," Shelby admitted.

Wait. Did that mean I was right? It was Ms. Lyons! Or Kaitlin!

"But how—"

Shelby cut me off. "Patience, Watson. Patience."

"This is so very exciting!" Shelby's mom exclaimed as she caught up to us.

I forced a smile since Shelby and I were currently under the guise of going over to our good friend's apartment for a sleepover. Nothing more.

As we walked, superheroes, princesses, and yes, ghosts and zombies surrounded us. Kids were running around comparing how full their Halloween bags were.

Oh, to be a normal kid right now.

The rest of the guys did decide to go out dressed up as zombies, while Bryant would spend the night with his dad in Brooklyn and I would stay at his apartment where Shelby and I would confront something . . . or someone. Possibly a ghost of some dead guy. (Because Shelby had still not proven that the ghost and beast didn't exist.)

This was such a bad idea.

"I'm so grateful for you, John," Mr. Holmes said as he put his arm around me, and I tried to not jump. I'd been super agitated all day since *I had no clue what was going on.* Oh, and *we were in danger!!* "You've done wonders for our Shelby."

"Yes!" Mrs. Holmes said. "And Shelby, I'm proud of you for making friends. I know how challenging that can be for you."

Shelby clenched her jaw, but remained uncharacteristically silent after her parents joined us. I didn't think she trusted her ability to keep up the charade if she opened her mouth. Her parents always seemed to test her boundaries.

Her mother looked at her father, who gave a nod. "And well," Mrs. Holmes began. "As a treat for this very special occasion, we are allowing you to have three pieces of Halloween candy tonight."

"How generous," Shelby replied with a smirk.

I had to bite my tongue so I wouldn't laugh. Shelby

already had over a dozen mini-Twix bars . . . *before* school. I remembered, because she was too busy eating to tell me what we had gotten ourselves into.

As we turned the corner to Bryant's place, the block seemed even darker and quieter than normal.

"My, so many empty buildings," Mrs. Holmes remarked as we passed by building after building of boarded-up windows and doors.

"Yes, this neighborhood is certainly changing," Mr. Holmes replied. "I can't necessarily say it's for the better. Harlem used to be fairly affordable, but all these developers keep buying up blocks like this."

They both shook their heads.

I looked around the block with a closer eye and noticed that the only building without a Sold sign—and with lights on—was Baskerville Estates.

I guess that's why Shelby wanted to do research about gentrification and real estate when we were at the library. It looked like Bryant's block was next.

We were rung up to Bryant's apartment, where he and his mom were waiting for us.

The parents did their flurry of introductions. Mr. and Mrs. Holmes were stumbling over themselves to thank Bryant's mom for having Shelby.

Huh. This might be the first time Shelby's parents had

one of their kids stay at someone else's house. Michael certainly wasn't the sleepover type. This was new to them as well.

Although let's be real: they were probably excited to have a night away from Shelby. Yeah, she was their daughter and all, but she was also a lot. A LOT.

Shelby stood off to the side as the parents kept talking, a smile frozen on her face. It looked unnatural on her, but she was trying.

I glanced at Bryant, who remained on the couch with his arms crossed.

He appeared to be in actual physical pain as his mom kept complimenting Shelby's violin playing.

Those two. How hard was it for them to pretend to get along for two minutes?

"Hey, man," I said to Bryant in an attempt to erase the glower on his face.

"Hey," he replied.

"Excited for tonight?" I said, overflowing with fake enthusiasm. I couldn't believe nobody called me on it.

"Yeah, sure," he said with so much dread there was no way anybody was going to buy that we were just three friends hanging for the night.

Bryant better not blow this. He and Shelby were going to have to play nice for the next few minutes.

Oddly enough, pretending to be Bryant's friend may be Shelby Holmes's greatest challenge. I mean, her pretending to be friends with anybody was a stretch. And this was coming from her one and only real friend.

It wasn't going to be so easy for Bryant, either. Man, the two of them were incredibly stubborn. It was shocking they weren't actually friends.

"And Bryant!" Mrs. Holmes extended her arms to Bryant. "It is so lovely to meet another one of Shelby's friends. You are such a wonderful violin player!"

"Thank you," Bryant said without much enthusiasm.

The parents looked between Shelby and Bryant, who were standing about as far apart as you could in the tiny apartment.

"Yeah, ah," I stumbled, trying to fix this situation ASAP. "We've been talking about doing this for a while. So cool of you to let Shelby come over, Mr. and Mrs. Holmes."

I nudged Shelby. She looked at me with a glare. I motioned over at Bryant. Shelby wasn't getting my hint.

"Talk to him," I mouthed.

Shelby grimaced as she approached Bryant. She sighed heavily.

Yep, it was going real, real well.

"What's up, Bryant?" Shelby then hit Bryant on the shoulder. By the way Bryant winced, I had to presume it was a little harder than a normal tap a buddy does. "I am, like, *so excited* to hang tonight."

Oh no. So here's the problem: Shelby knew how to be a different person, but she forgot that she was still supposed to be herself. Shelby Holmes didn't say "What's up" or "like." She spoke with purpose. And if I was to be honest, as if she were a four-hundred-year-old college professor with no sense of humor.

"Ah, yeah." Bryant rubbed his shoulder. "Me too."

"Splendid!" Shelby clapped her hands. "Well, *buddy*, shall we get to it!" She then turned to her parents.

"Oh! Yes! We should be going," Mrs. Holmes replied with the same clap. The difference was hers was genuine. "Claire and John, I hope you both can join us for dinner some night. It would be delightful to get to know Shelby's friends better."

Bryant's mouth dropped open, while his mother graciously accepted. She seemed to genuinely like the Holmeses. Most people did. It was their children that were a little . . . ah, challenging.

With all the risks of this case, nobody could foresee whether Bryant's mom and Shelby's parents would become friends. If that happened, it would be a miracle if Bryant or Shelby could survive.

"Shelby!" Her mom enveloped her in a giant hug with

her father joining them. "We are going to miss you so much. Please call if you need anything or want to come home."

"We know this is a big step for you," her father said.

Oh wow. WOW. I'd been thinking about Shelby's parents, but I didn't realize that this was Shelby's first night away from them. Maybe there was a time her parents went somewhere and she had a babysitter (that poor, poor babysitter), but this was new ground for her, too.

Shelby didn't seem to be that bothered by it as she wiggled out of her parents' embrace. "I do not foresee a scenario where communications would be required."

Ah, *there's* the Shelby we all know.

Shelby's parents gave another round of thanks before they left.

The room was quiet for a few beats before Shelby turned to Bryant and his mom. "My gratitude for having to endure that charade. I must ask that you wait a few more minutes before you depart, as I'm sure my parents are still outside. They have separation anxiety."

"Whatever you need," Bryant's mom said as she went into the kitchen.

Bryant looked down at the floor. "So, you know, thanks for this."

"You can thank us when the case is solved," Shelby replied curtly.

I glared at Shelby. Bryant was trying. Sort of.

"Yeah, so," Bryant started as his foot shook. "I just want you guys to be careful. I don't want anything to happen to you."

"We'll be careful, man," I assured him.

"Yes, let's not get mushy. Watson and I will be fine," Shelby replied before cautiously approaching the window. She stepped to the side as she pulled back the blinds. "As I suspected, my parents are still out there."

"Are you *sure* you're going to be okay?" Bryant's mom asked.

"Yeah, we've got a plan and everything," I stated, even though Shelby had yet to fully fill me in.

"And more importantly, we'll be able to wrap up this case," Shelby added.

Ah, *that* was more important than our safety?

This wasn't going to end well. I had a feeling.

"My parents are finally departing. At their average walking rate, they should be around the corner and on Lenox in fifty-five seconds." Shelby held up her watch.

Average walking rate? Why did that surprise me?

"Be careful," Bryant's mom said with a worried look on her face. "And if at any point you don't feel safe, please leave or call the police."

Shelby grimaced. "As I've stated, we'll be fine. You have

my assurances. As Watson can attest, my word is the best guarantee you can be given."

Egotistical? Yeah.

True? Yep.

"Thanks for everything," Bryant said as he ran his hands through his shaggy hair. "I, um, appreciate it. But my mom's right—get out if you're in danger."

"We will," I said since I was planning on running out the second anything got too scary.

Bryant's mom gave us both a hug, and Shelby didn't cringe too much. With one final nod of his head, Bryant followed his mom out the door.

Now Shelby and I were the only ones left in this building. Allegedly.

Shelby turned to me with a giddy expression on her face. "Now that those unpleasantries are over with, it's time we get to work."

"Okay, what's first?" I asked, trying to psych myself up for this.

"We're going to set a little trap."

~CHAPTER~
26

WE WERE HIDING.

And it smelled.

Really smelled.

"Stop fidgeting," Shelby hissed at me as we were squeezed into the little nook next to the building. The one where Kaitlin smoked. Not only were we standing on a scattering of cigarette butts, but behind us was a small metal fence lined with garbage cans.

It was disgusting.

Something scurried past my foot. I held in a scream; I was pretty sure it was a rat.

I didn't know what to think. All I did know was that I couldn't wait for us to get out of this space, but that meant we'd have to deal with whoever we were waiting for.

"Can't you at least tell me who?" I asked.

Shelby looked perplexed. "Whatever for? You already know who, Watson. It was you who figured it out."

I figured it out?

What did—

Oh no.

No. No. *NO.*

That couldn't mean—

I didn't even want to think it.

Shelby nudged me gently, which meant one thing.

The suspect was coming.

Oh, how I wished I was wrong.

Before I could properly prepare myself, Shelby quietly stepped out from hiding and I reluctantly followed.

And there she was.

Moira Hardy.

Yep. MOIRA HARDY.

WHY? Why was it when I was right about something— and let's not forget figuring something out before Shelby— it had to be about Moira!

Crud.

My mind swirled about WHY she was involved and HOW, but I also felt pretty proud of myself for realizing she was entangled in this mess. Even though that meant we had to confront her.

Moira didn't see us sneak behind her. She had her usual tidy high ponytail, but instead of her Miss Adler's School for Girls uniform, she wore black from head to toe. She used a key to open the front door of Baskerville Estates.

Shelby cleared her throat loudly.

Moira fumbled with the door, which then shut. As she turned around, her face had a neutral expression.

"Good evening, Moira," Shelby said evenly. "Funny running into you here."

"Well, well, if it isn't the somewhat adequate Shelby Holmes and her sidekick, John Watson," she said with a smirk.

Ugh. Moira really was the worst.

First, I was not a sidekick. Okay, I took the lead from Shelby, but I also did things on my own.

Moira flipped her ponytail. "I'm not at all surprised to see you."

"You've made it quite evident you were involved in this silly farce," Shelby said with her arms crossed.

She had? I was only going off the fact that this was precisely the kind of thing Moira liked to do and could fit the description of the person who gave Kaitlin the note. But that was a pretty big stretch.

A pretty big stretch that was dead on.

Moira laughed lightly. "Oh, really? What tipped you off?"

Shelby gestured at me. "It was Watson who deduced not only that the article was a sham but that you were the one who dropped off that letter."

Nice! Shelby was giving me the credit!

"Did you enjoy getting to be me for a few minutes?" Shelby asked as she circled Moira near the window of Barrymore's apartment. "Although even on your best day, you'd be a poor facsimile."

Moira wrinkled her nose. "No surprise that being you felt as subpar as one could be."

Seriously. These two.

They'd probably be the closest of friends if they didn't despise each other so much.

"Some of your antics have been quite clever," Shelby admitted. "Yet I'm aware you are only pulling the strings here."

Moira studied her nails, as if she was bored by this conversation. "You aren't the only one who can offer her services."

Moira has clients now? What do people do to get ahold of her? Call 1-800-PURE-EVIL.

She turned her attention to me and I froze.

"I see you're still hanging around with this amateur, Watson." Moira gave me a sinister smile. "If you ever want a real challenge, you should come work with me. I'd give you lots of interesting things to write about."

"Ah, no thanks," I replied while Shelby grimaced.

No thanks? Come on, Watson. You can do better!

"I'd never work with you!" I declared as I stood tall. "Shelby is smarter than you'll ever be. We're going to figure out what you're up to and end this. Just like we ended things with you before."

Moira narrowed her eyes at me. "Oh, you have some fight in you. I admire that. I didn't get a chance to ask you how that ambulance ride was from when we previously crossed paths."

I opened my mouth and then closed it. There was no reasoning with evil.

Shelby stood between Moira and me. "You even give Watson the common cold and I will descend upon you with a fury unlike you've ever seen."

Whoa. Shelby did not play. A lump got caught in my throat. I knew Shelby would never let Moira get the better of us again, but still.

"And how was that volunteering you had to do after our last encounter?" Shelby asked with a smirk as Moira recoiled slightly. "I'm sure you enjoyed cleaning up parks and having to scrub graffiti off walls."

Moira replied by slitting her eyes at Shelby.

"I'm here to inform you that your services are no longer needed." Shelby crossed her arms.

Moira batted her eyelashes. "I don't know what you're talking about."

"You just asked us how we knew!" I stated, and then closed my mouth.

"Know about what? I'm simply out for Halloween."

"Dressed as what, a witch?" Shelby fired at her. "But then again you wouldn't need a costume for that, would you?"

I let out a laugh. Man, Shelby really was working on her humor. And that *was* funny. Unlike telling me that a serial killer had keys to my apartment. So she could learn! (About being a better person; we already knew she could learn about anything and everything book-related.)

"Tell me, who has keys for trick-or-treating?" Shelby asked.

Moira put the keys behind her back, like that was going to fool us. "That proves nothing."

"If you're so innocent you wouldn't mind us looking into your bag." Shelby gestured at Moira's oversized black backpack.

Moira lifted her chin. "Do you have a warrant?"

"Only guilty people demand warrants," Shelby stated as she held out her hand. "If you don't have anything to hide."

"As if you can tell me what I can and cannot do. Nobody can." Moira gave a little laugh that turned into a sigh.

"I think your parents would disagree with that." Moira flinched slightly. "But there's someone else who can poke holes through that theory of yours."

Moira scoffed. "Who? You? You have no proof I've done anything wrong."

Ah, besides the fact that she just said she offered her services. But it would be our word against hers. And as we discovered last time, her parents' money and influence spoke louder than the truth.

"No. The police." Shelby nodded down the deserted street, and a black sedan flashed its lights.

Wait. WHAT?

I tried to keep my face neutral so Moira couldn't tell that I was in the dark about what was going on.

Shelby continued, "That is Detective Lestrade of the New York City Police Department. You may recall her from outside your apartment building? She's been called in about the disturbances here. If you proceed into Baskerville Estates she's going to have some questions for you. As you're a minor, she'll have no choice but to call your parents in. Then again, maybe that will give you the attention you so desperately crave since you continue to fumble when it comes to besting me."

Moira glanced up at the building. "You have no idea what you've gotten yourself into." She sneered with anger. "You may think you've won, but you haven't. This is about more than me. You are so in over your head."

Shelby yawned. "I think it's you that is in over her head." Shelby then clapped. "Well, I'd say it was lovely speaking with you, Moira, but I leave deception to those with lesser talents." Shelby turned to me and said very loudly, "I don't know about you, Watson, but I'm relieved to have this all behind us. Let's go into the apartment for an enjoyable evening of watching movies and eating candy. You may go."

She waved Moira away.

Wait. That was it? It was over? Just like that?

But— But— But—

I had so many questions, but I kept my mouth shut as I knew Shelby had a plan.

Moira laughed. She had an evil cackle—it sent chills down my spine.

"Oh yes, have a wonderful evening," Moira replied. "But make no mistake, you'll see me again."

"I'm looking forward to it," Shelby replied. And I kid you not, she really did seem like she couldn't wait to see Moira again. Shelby actually liked coming face-to-face with her. Moira was an admirable sparring partner for Shelby. While I preferred to stick to dognappers and vengeful figure skaters. "Even though outsmarting you is starting to become quite pedestrian."

Moira glared and opened her mouth to say something, but glanced at Lestrade's headlights and thought better of it. She then turned down the street.

I had too many questions for Shelby, but she held up her hand, signaling that she didn't want me to talk. I didn't understand why. The sidewalk was deserted. We waited for Moira to turn the corner, then Shelby nodded at Lestrade, who started her car and went down the street.

"Well, Watson," Shelby said loudly. "I'm so happy to have another case solved."

She began typing into her phone.

"So . . . we're done?" It seemed a little anticlimactic. Although all we really knew now was that Moira was involved. There were so many unanswered questions. There's no way this was that simple.

"Yes!" Shelby replied as she headed back into the building.

My phone beeped. It was a text from Shelby, **We are just getting started.**

That's what I was afraid of.

CHAPTER 27

SHELBY WALKED AROUND BRYANT'S APARTMENT TURNING ON a bunch of lights.

"What on earth is going on?" I asked quietly. "How did *you* know Moira was involved?"

Shelby reached into her back pocket and pulled out the fake *New York Times* article about Hugo Baskerville. "Remember how I said it's all in the details? Well, I did not listen to my own advice and simply disregarded the article without properly studying it."

I stared blankly back at her.

She tapped at the reporter's name, Mara I. Rhody. "Moira basically signed the article."

I stared at the name and it started to come together. "Oh, wow."

It was in front of us all this time.

Mara I. Rhody was an anagram for Moira Hardy.

"It's a little uninspiring if you ask me," Shelby said

with a sniff. "Moira is far too clever for such amateur antics."

"Okay, but *why* is she involved?"

"As she stated, she has a client."

"But who is her client? How?" That still didn't explain everything that had been happening in an empty apartment. I still wasn't 100 percent certain that Hugo Baskerville was completely at rest. Dude did die in that apartment. "And you brought in Lestrade?"

Shelby's face scrunched up. "It was becoming rather obvious this was a complex web that required the police's involvement."

She didn't like to admit she needed help from anybody, especially Lestrade.

"So is Lestrade going to arrest her?" I asked, hopeful.

"No, she's simply making sure Moira leaves the area."

I felt defeated. "She's going to get away with it."

"Of course not." Shelby reached into her jacket pocket and pulled out her cell phone. "I recorded our conversation downstairs. We have her admitting to having a client and being involved. Lestrade witnessed her trying to enter the building. At this juncture, we need Moira to *think* she's gotten away with it. Therefore she can alert her client that she won't be able to participate in tonight's festivities and the client will have to take over."

I sat down on a chair, my mind still trying to connect the dots. I let out a groan.

"Oh, Watson, you shouldn't be so disgruntled when we're so close to solving this."

We were? Because I was more confused than ever.

"For the next couple hours, the most important thing is to never relax your precautions," she instructed. Which was fine and all, but I had no idea what that meant. Shelby sighed as she took in my confused expression. "Stay alert."

I let out a laugh. "Um, Shelby, I don't think it's possible for me to be any more alert." That was an understatement. I was still on edge from seeing Moira. Now it was super quiet in the building and we were supposed to wait for something to happen. It was like when you watched a scary movie and you tense up waiting for someone to jump out. And kill someone.

Have I mentioned what a bad idea this was?

"Great!" Shelby headed for the door. "I'll be right back. Feel free to be as loud as possible. Turn on the TV. Walk around."

"Where are you going?" No way was I going to let her leave me alone in here. Not like I could ever get Shelby to do anything.

"Just setting one crucial piece of our puzzle in motion. I will be back in less than two minutes." She then closed the door. Leaving me by myself.

Okay, I knew that this place really couldn't be haunted. But did I really?

Again, we didn't have answers for everything that was happening in an empty apartment.

I also had no idea how we were going to capture this person. Or thing.

Please don't have it be a beast. Pretty please.

But let's be real, I did know one thing for sure: Shelby had a plan.

She also had to have a suspect. She didn't say I was wrong about Ms. Lyons or Kaitlin.

Shelby came back, walking with a little more purpose. "Let's watch a movie. A scary movie," she said loudly.

When I opened my mouth to reply, she nodded, signaling me to be quiet. She walked over until she was only an inch from my ear. "I need there to be a presumption that we are in for the evening." She turned on the TV and flipped the channels until she settled on some slasher flick. Awesome. Just awesome. She turned up the volume.

"Once I realized Moira was involved, I knew I couldn't underestimate her again. Which is why I had to bring Lestrade in. We, unfortunately, aren't done needing her assistance tonight."

Shelby handed me a piece of paper with letterhead on it that said Hardy Enterprises.

"What?"

"Moira made this personal, which is why it was rather easy to catch her. She had to taunt us with that note and use my name. She's so ego-driven she had to use an anagram of her name in that article. She wanted to get credit for this because it would get her points with her father."

"What?" I repeated. "So her dad is the client?"

Shelby shook her head. "Not exactly."

"Wait a second, wouldn't Moira tell her client we were on to her?" There was no way Moira would just let this go.

Shelby nodded. "I'm counting on it. I wanted Moira to be under the assumption that we think the case is closed and we wouldn't be ready for what's about to come."

"What's about to come?" I asked with dread.

Shelby glanced at her watch. "We don't have a lot of time. The power should go out soon. I went and cleaned the fuse box so I can dust for fingerprints afterward. That is the most logical reason for the power going out. Tonight we need to gather all the evidence to cement our case."

Shelby grabbed her backpack. "Now we must be very quiet." She tiptoed to the door.

"What?" I whispered as I followed her by carefully crossing the living room. "Where are we going?"

"We aren't staying here," Shelby remarked.

Finally! Maybe Shelby realized how crazy this plan was.

"We're going upstairs to hide in apartment five."

Oh, Watson. Poor, poor Watson. Of course things were about to get worse.

Of course they were.

Happy Halloween to me.

CHAPTER
28

THERE WE WERE. OUTSIDE THE ROOM WHERE, AH, SOMETHING was going on.

Before I could ask how we'd get inside, Shelby produced two keys. "Did you get those from Mr. Barrymore?"

Shelby shook her head. "No, I acquired them the good old-fashioned way."

Which meant that she'd stolen the keys at some point. I raced my mind back through the last two days.

Before I could ask her, she replied, "While you were all distracted by that note from Moira, I slipped them out of his pocket."

"Wouldn't he know they're missing?" I asked.

"These are copies," Shelby replied as the door clicked open. "I made an impression of the keys with putty, and returned them to him within seconds."

She did all of that under all our noses.

Maybe I really was a sidekick.

Sigh.

Shelby closed the door quietly behind us. I took a few hesitant steps, but I got that weird feeling again. I didn't feel steady.

"Shelby," I said as I balanced on my foot. "This doesn't feel right."

While I didn't have that feeling of dread like before, I felt off balance, which didn't fill me with a feeling of assurance that this could all be explained away.

That feeling only really happened in this unit.

That could not be a good sign.

"You're correct. I'll show you why later." She reached into her backpack and pulled out two flashlights. "We have to hurry. The last few nights have followed a pattern: lights are cut, followed by the footsteps, then tapping and howling."

"Okay, so what's the plan?"

"Since Moira isn't able to cause the noise, the person she's working for will have to do it. So we're going to hide and let the perp come to us."

I looked around the empty room. Where were we going to hide? The closet? In one of the bedrooms? Because let me make something clear: there was no way, and I mean *no way*, I was going to hide in the shower. That screamed horror movie scenario.

Shelby began running her hand around the wall next to the kitchen.

"What are you doing?" I asked.

"This area has a significantly smaller square footage than the unit downstairs."

Hey! I also thought that when we first came up here, but I blamed the absence of furniture. It really was smaller. But what did that mean?

"There was a reason when we came in here we didn't see Moira. She was hiding where she couldn't be found if you didn't know where to look."

At that moment, the lights flickered.

"Turn on the flashlights," Shelby instructed as she continued to feel around the wall. "Aha!" she exclaimed as she pushed the wall. There was a clicking noise, and the wall popped open, revealing a secret room.

Then the lights went out. The apartment was completely dark, save for the beam of our two flashlights.

"Get in!" Shelby instructed. We both squeezed inside the tiny space. "We have to shut off the lights."

If I thought it was dark in the living room, in the secret room I couldn't see anything.

"Now we wait," Shelby whispered.

"For what?" I asked. I hated being left in the dark—literally and figuratively—but I also knew Shelby didn't tell me the whole plan because she deduced I wouldn't be cool if she said, *"Hey, Watson, we're going to lock ourselves in a possibly haunted room where we'll be trapped and it'll be pitch black."*

So being left in the dark it was.

I didn't want to know what was next.

"We're waiting for him to fall for our trap."

It was a him! It wasn't Ms. Lyons or Kaitlin! It was Mr. Stapleton!

But wait a second. "I thought you said my deductions about Ms. Lyons and Kaitlin were logical."

"They were, but that didn't signify they were correct."

Before I could say anything else, we heard it.

Those footsteps.

And they were coming closer.

CHAPTER
29

Oh no. There it was.

STOMP.

Whoooosh.

STOMP.

Whoooosh.

STOMP.

Whoooosh.

Even though we were hidden away, the sound was the loudest I've ever heard it. We were only a few feet away from whoever was doing this, on the other side of this door.

I tensed, waiting for it. Not like the footsteps weren't bad enough. It was the anticipation of the howl that was the worst.

HOOOOOOWWWWL!

I shuddered. I almost jumped when I felt Shelby's hand in mine. She gave me a squeeze.

Was Shelby actually scared?

Oh wow.

Although let's be real: Shelby was probably holding my hand because she knew I was freaking out. She gave another squeeze. Was she signaling me? Oh please don't tell me she was passing on some secret Morse code message to me, because I hadn't been able to fully memorize the whole alphabet, much to Shelby's annoyance. I had schoolwork. And journal writing. And apparently a secret room to hide in.

The light from Shelby's phone lit up her face. She typed with one hand and then put her phone away.

As the hound howled away and started scraping at . . . something (please don't let it be this door), we heard another set of footsteps. These were farther away and seemed to be coming up the stairs.

The howling suddenly stopped, and the entrance to the secret room flung open. A flashlight blinded us, so I couldn't see who held it, but he let out a gasp in surprise upon seeing us before dropping the flashlight.

The flashlight clattered on the floor, and the person chased after it while I could only look on. We stood in the room with the person responsible for everything. Even though it was two against one, this person was bigger than us. And we were trapped.

He finally grabbed the flashlight and put it back in our faces so we couldn't get a good look at him.

I held up my hand over my eyes to prevent being blinded by the light.

Shelby stepped out of the room with confidence. "Happy Halloween, Mr. Barrymore."

⌐·CHAPTER·⌐
30

WHAT? BARRYMORE?

But . . . but . . . but . . .

I wasn't the only one confused.

Mr. Barrymore pointed his finger at us, his hands shaking. "It was you? You—You must've—You could've—"

He was going to try to blame this on us? Yeah, nice try.

A knock on the door rattled both Mr. Barrymore and me. Shelby remained as cool as ever.

"Maybe you should get that?" she suggested.

Mr. Barrymore looked between the door and us. "I don't know what you're playing at."

His eyes narrowed as he walked over to the door. Before Barrymore opened it, I had a feeling I knew who'd be on the other side.

And yep, there she was, standing in the darkness of the hallway with a flashlight shining up so her face was illuminated: Detective Lestrade.

"Thank you for coming promptly, Detective Lestrade," Shelby said coolly. "This conversation might be better accompanied by light, even though I will be the one illuminating everybody on these recent matters."

"I'll do it," Mr. Barrymore said, but Lestrade put her hand on the frame of the door.

"Not so fast. We wouldn't want you to interfere with a key piece of evidence," Lestrade stated.

So Lestrade knew about Shelby's plan to clean the fuse box.

She turned to exit the room, but paused. "Maybe I shouldn't leave you two alone with him."

Shelby snorted. "I think we've proven to be quite capable."

Lestrade pointed her flashlight at Barrymore. "Do not move an inch until I return." She gave Shelby a nod as she climbed back down the stairs.

Barrymore wrung his hands while we waited in silence for Lestrade to return. Shelby went to the kitchen counter and started to lay out files.

The lights in the apartment came on again suddenly. I blinked for a moment while my eyes adjusted.

"I don't know what you think you're doing," Barrymore said, his voice high. He looked nervous.

He looked guilty.

Shelby crossed her arms as we heard Lestrade on the stairs.

After Lestrade walked in, she removed plastic gloves. "Okay, Holmes. Talk."

"With pleasure!" Shelby picked up the first file folder and handed it to Lestrade. "Mr. Barrymore here has been trying to get rid of his tenants so he could sell this apartment building he inherited from his uncle. As you can see from these plans, the entire block has been bought up by a developer to build a new luxury condo building. The developer is one Hardy Enterprises, which just happens to be where Mr. Barrymore has his internship."

Barrymore interned at Hardy Enterprises?

The plot thickened.

"Mr. Barrymore wasn't able to force his tenants out as his uncle had put a provision in the leases that tenants would be given three years' notice before being forced to vacate. The senior Barrymore appeared not to like what was happening to his beloved neighborhood. To put it plainly: Barrymore wanted to sell the building to make a lot of money, but his uncle made it impossible to kick his tenants out. Therefore, he needed to give them a reason to want to vacate immediately."

Oh.

OH.

There was the motive. The WHY.

We had the WHO.

Now I knew what was next. Shelby would explain HOW he did it.

Shelby began pacing the room while Lestrade took her notebook out and furiously scribbled down everything Shelby had just said. Barrymore, meanwhile, looked like he was going to be sick.

"I do have to compliment you, Barrymore," Shelby said. "It was quite a clever plan, albeit a dangerous one. One that I believe you didn't come up with yourself."

Mr. Barrymore looked like he was the one who saw a ghost.

"I'll take that as a yes," she continued. "No doubt he met his chicanery coconspirator at his internship—more on her shortly. First, how did they convince the tenants there was something wrong? They used carbon monoxide to give the tenants an uneasy and paranoid feeling. Barrymore removed the batteries of all the carbon monoxide detectors in their units. The dosage was small enough not to poison them, but it still affected the elderly Mr. Mortimer. By the time they stopped using the carbon monoxide, the seed had already been planted with the tenants.

The next part is quite simple: Barrymore turned the power off on the fuse box, while his coconspirator walked around this unit that Barrymore intentionally kept empty.

They used a recording device to play the sound of a wild beast howling. A device you'll no doubt find on Barrymore now if you search him. They added scratching noises and the tapping in Morse code to really rev up the tension. When we went into this unit, the person making the noise hid in the secret compartment."

Shelby walked over to the counter and pulled out another folder. "Now let's look at this Baskerville legend. One Mr. Hugo Baskerville did die in this very unit one hundred years ago, but from a fall. Not murder, as you'll see from this *New York Times* obituary from November 2, 1919." Shelby put the real article I found on the counter, alongside the fake one. "A tour guide gave us this phony article that talked about haunting and a beast. He can attest that Mr. Barrymore hired him. You may call him to confirm it yourself." Shelby handed Lestrade the guy's head shot.

Lestrade flipped through the papers in the file. "How did you get all of this?"

"Simple, the library," Shelby stated. "You also may have realized that the fake article reporter's name is an anagram for Barrymore's coconspirator, one Moira Hardy. I have her on tape confessing to being part of this."

Shelby held up her phone and typed in it for a few seconds before Lestrade's cell phone dinged.

Lestrade looked up from the folder. "I knew that girl

I followed looked familiar. Moira Hardy? Where do I know that name?" Then her eyes got wide. "Oh, from . . ." She shook her head as she looked at me.

"Yes, a worthy foe if there ever was one," Shelby said with a smile. An actual, legit smile.

"It looks like I'll be having a talk with her and her parents when we're done here," Lestrade stated.

YES! So Moira wouldn't get away with it. ABOUT TIME!

"Shall I go on?" Shelby asked Lestrade.

"Please, do," Lestrade said with a nod of awe.

Barrymore put his hand on the counter to steady himself.

"They used claw marks and fake blood, which we found in this unit, to really make the tenants uneasy. But I do have to say my favorite part of this ruse is below us."

Bryant's apartment?

Shelby walked with a little more purpose across the floor. "As you may notice, it's not stable. It gives you the sense, especially if the power is cut, that you aren't balanced."

Lestrade bobbled a little. "You're right. I did notice it, but I have no idea why."

Shelby reached into her backpack and pulled out a crowbar. "May I?" she asked Lestrade with a raised eyebrow.

"No!" Barrymore cried out as he put his head in his hands.

Lestrade stepped back.

Shelby got on her knees, took the crowbar to the wooden floor, and cracked open one of the floorboards. She put on plastic gloves of her own before she reached down and pulled out a couple of . . . golf balls?

"If you put these close together and place a board on top, it gives about a half inch of movement, just enough to make one feel uneasy. I believe this had to be a Moira touch."

We all turned to Mr. Barrymore, his head dropped. But he did give a little nod.

"Genius!" Shelby replied with a clap. "Yes, this was a very solid plan, indeed, Mr. Barrymore. Especially to coincide with Halloween, a holiday where paranoia and paranormal delusions run rampant."

All the clues from the last few days began to swirl in my head. "What about the letter given to Barrymore? The one that was allegedly from you?"

"Ah, yes!" said Shelby. "That letter was to throw us off Barrymore's scent. Moira must have realized that one of the tenants went to the Harlem Academy of the Arts, and therefore deduced that you and I would eventually become aware of these odd occurrences. It's probably one of the reasons she wanted to take on this case. While Moira no doubt enjoyed dressing up as me, that bit made it very clear that this was all a ruse. How could a spirit deliver a letter? So you no doubt will want to thank your accomplice for that, Mr. Barrymore."

Barrymore's entire demeanor was defeated.

"You didn't account for two things when you tried to mess with your tenants," Shelby said. "One, people in Harlem take care of their own. And two, never, ever underestimate the intelligence of kids, especially ones as smart as Watson and me."

Barrymore remained silent. I think we all were stunned with the amount of information—and cold, hard evidence—Shelby had presented.

"I just . . ." Mr. Barrymore finally spoke, in a soft voice. "I never wanted this building. I'm only twenty-four. I'm in business school. I wanted to get rid of it, and a developer from Hardy Enterprises contacted me. They offered me a lot of money for the building. They became aggressive and gave me a dream internship. Then I got a message from this anonymous person offering to help me out. I didn't know most of the plan. She kept me in the dark. I had no idea about that letter. I don't know this Moira you're talking about as she never gave me her name. She made sure we never crossed paths. She always hid in the secret room when I came up. Did you say . . . she's also a girl? Like you?"

Shelby snorted. "A girl? Yes. Like me? She could only dream."

Barrymore sunk his head. "I never meant for anybody to get hurt. I just thought people would get spooked and want to move. That was all. It got out of hand, but it was too late. And my contact . . . well, she wouldn't back down. There was nothing I could've done."

"You could've told the truth," Shelby countered. She then turned to Lestrade. "I believe you have everything you need."

Lestrade nodded. "Yes. I do." She looked at the folders in her hand. "Thank you, Holmes."

"You're welcome, Lestrade."

Okay, Barrymore wasn't the only one stunned by the turn of events. Was this an official truce between Lestrade and Shelby? Would we be calling her for all our cases?

"Someone had to do the police's work," Shelby replied with a sniff.

And truce over.

Lestrade grimaced as she took Barrymore by the arm and escorted him out of the apartment unit.

"Well, Watson, you can call your friend. It's safe to come home."

~CHAPTER~
31

"TIMING IS EVERYTHING," SHELBY SAID THE NEXT DAY AS WE left school.

Bryant stood outside with a duffel bag at his feet.

"Hey," Bryant said as he kicked the sidewalk. "My mom dropped this off for you. The rest of our neighbors will be delivering their thanks later today. Even Mr. Mortimer, who was released from the hospital this morning."

"Wonderful!" Shelby replied as she opened the bag.

Do you even need one guess of what's inside?

Yep, candy.

Bags and bags of Halloween candy.

A lightbulb went off in my head. Because it was now on sale with Halloween being over. *That's* what Shelby meant about timing.

"And this is for you, Watson." Bryant handed me a gift card for Sal's pizzeria. "Thanks for everything."

"Sweet! Thank you!"

Bryant looked down at the sidewalk. "We're really grateful you guys figured it out. Mr. Stapleton is looking into buying the building so we can all stay there."

"That's awesome!" I replied.

Shelby put an entire mini-bag of M&M's in her mouth.

"I still can't believe everything Barrymore and that

Moira girl did just to scare us. Oh, hey, I did have one more question for you: How did they get the candles to keep going out?"

"What?" Shelby said with her face scrunched up.

Oh, yeah. The candles blew out shortly after the lights went out.

Both Bryant and I looked to Shelby, waiting for her to explain.

She stared blankly at us for a second. "A simple breeze."

"Oh, okay, yeah, I guess that makes sense," Bryant said with a shrug of his shoulders.

Um, wait a second. What breeze? From where? I didn't feel a breeze—

Stop it, Watson. As Shelby proved, there was no such thing as ghosts.

Well, at least in Bryant's apartment building. Allegedly.

Bryant kicked the sidewalk again. I noticed it was something he did when he was uncomfortable. "And Shelby, thanks for helping. I know we aren't that close, and well, it was really cool to watch you in action. I really appreciate what you did."

"Your expression of gratitude has been accepted," she stated as she held up the candy. "I realize how excruciating this must be for you, so you may move on."

She motioned her hand at Bryant to go away.

I nudged Shelby and gave her a look. The one my mom would give me if I needed to straighten up my act.

Shelby grimaced. "You're welcome, Bryant. I was most happy to be of assistance to you and your neighbors." Then Shelby turned to me. "Is that acceptable?"

I mean, I guess that was as much as I could expect with those two.

"Yeah, okay. So I'll see you in class," Bryant said before waving us goodbye.

"Yes, until then." And I swear, she gave him the hint of a smile.

Maybe there was hope for them yet.

"Shelby," I began.

"Watson," Shelby cut me off. "Is your friend not a satisfied client? Did we not get to the bottom of his problem?"

"Yeah, but—"

"Yes, I could be friendlier. Unlike you, I don't like to muddy the waters with feelings. Look what happened with Moira when she made things personal. She ended up being careless."

I sighed. Every time I thought I was getting somewhere with her regarding people, she'd take eighteen giant steps back.

"But, Watson, I don't need to be the friendly one—that's your specialty."

"That doesn't make me special. Most people treat others with respect."

Shelby snorted. "Since when?"

I shook my head. Shelby put her arm around my shoulder. "Watson, you know I could never do this without you. You center me. You sometimes see things that I can't, especially when human emotions are involved. So thank you."

Wow. Maybe I was making progress. Even if it was just Shelby being kinder to me. I was going to take any small victory I could.

"Are we okay?" Shelby asked.

"Yeah." We had solved another case. Bryant was going to be able to stay in his home. "We're cool."

Because no matter how abrupt Shelby was, she was my partner and my friend.

~·CHAPTER·~
32

"Here's to another successful case," Aisha said to me as she held up her glass of soda at Sal's on Saturday afternoon.

"And here's to competing at sectionals," I replied as our glasses clinked together.

Aisha smiled at me, and oh boy, my stomach did this weird flutter. "Thanks, I'm so glad we were able to do this, especially since I have to step up my training next week."

We looked down at our table covered with the crumbs from our lunch of garlic bread and pepperoni pizza. Last time I was here with Aisha, she could only have a small side salad since being a figure skater was no joke.

Okay, I also thought that she might've been sending bullying notes to her main rival.

(I sometimes wasn't the best judge of character when it came to our cases.)

Luckily, Aisha turned out to be innocent and yeah, I liked her. Maybe Mom wasn't the only person in the family who could date. Even though I was only eleven and so not ready to settle down or anything.

Not like this was a date.

Whatever.

"This is so good." Aisha closed her eyes as she finished her slice of pizza.

"Yeah, Sal's the best." I took one last bite, since I had to be careful about eating too much with my diabetes. Mom gave me permission to have two slices, and then I had to get my glucose levels checked when I got home.

I sank back in my seat. The case was over. I was spending my Saturday afternoon eating pizza with a cool girl. This new life wasn't all bad.

"I'm glad we were able to do this," I said as I took the check from Sal. I had Bryant's gift card burning a hole in my pocket. "My treat."

Aisha smiled at me before her eyes suddenly flew wide open.

"What is it?"

She tilted her head. "Is that your foot?"

"Is what my foot?" My feet were on the floor, not touching anything.

Both Aisha and I looked under the table at the same time.

She was the first to jump up and scream. I was quick to follow.

Because there—under our table—was a snake.

Let me repeat: there was a snake in a pizzeria.

"AH!" Aisha screamed as she jumped up on the table across from us. The other customers all looked on in alert.

"Watson!" Sal came rushing over. "What's wrong?"

I couldn't find my voice and could only point under the table, but then that familiar red hair popped up from the booth behind us. Shelby scooped up the snake in one arm. "Nothing to be alarmed about. A simple garden snake."

SHELBY?!?!

"Seriously?" Aisha said before she jumped down from the booth and ran out the door.

"What are you doing?" I scolded a confused Shelby as I ran out to follow Aisha.

"I'm so sorry!" I called after her. "I have no idea what's going on. But we can go back inside."

Aisha's skin was ashen. "No way can I go back in there! I hate snakes!"

Oh, man. Shelby was in so much trouble.

"I'm so sorry," I repeated. I didn't want this to be the way our really nice lunch ended. "Maybe we can go get ice cream or something. Get as far away from Sal's and that snake as possible. And Shelby."

Aisha shivered. "It's okay. I need to get home. Um . . ."

We both stood there. I didn't know how to make up for

Shelby's behavior. It was a position I was often in, but Aisha wasn't a client. She was a friend. A really cute one.

"I'm really, really sorry."

"Watson, you don't have to keep apologizing. *You* didn't do anything."

I knew that, but I was used to apologizing for Shelby.

"I know, but I feel bad. Really bad. So I'll talk to you later?" I didn't want this to be the last I saw of her.

"Yeah." She gave me a small smile and then gave me a hug. "I'll talk to you later."

I watched her walk away with a big smile on my face, a smile that vanished once I turned back to Sal's. I stormed into the pizzeria and saw that Shelby was beaming.

"Did it work?" she asked.

"Did what work? Oh, are you referring to trying to ruin my day?"

I mean, really?

Shelby's expression fell. "Oh, but the emotions for fear and love are closely related, so many times people can form romantic feelings for someone when they've been put in a frightening situation. There are many studies—"

"Shelby!" I cut her off. "Are you telling me you purposely scared Aisha so she would like me?"

"Of course," Shelby replied softly. "Isn't this what you told me friends do? They help each other out. You're my friend, I wanted to help you."

Unbelievable. I mean, it was kind of sweet when you think about it, but still. A snake. She thought *a snake* was going to make Aisha like me.

Not like I wanted anything like that to happen or anything.

Whatever.

"Is Aisha mad?" Shelby asked.

"What do you think?" I glowered at her.

"I'm sorry, Watson. I really am."

And I could see by her face that she meant it. She really did try to help me, and it backfired big time.

Shelby looked out the door. "She's not coming back?"

"No, she's not. We were almost done anyway." I took a few steps away from the bag in Shelby's hand that was moving.

The check wasn't on the table anymore.

"I took care of it," Shelby stated as she handed my gift card back. "It's the least I could do."

Ah, the least she could've done was to stay home and not pull that stunt.

"So what I did wasn't a friendly thing?" she asked, her forehead creased.

Being a friend was hard for Shelby. There wasn't a book she could study.

I put my arm around her. "Shelby, we might have to do some lessons about how to treat friends."

"But you're the only friend that matters, Watson."

Which was precisely why I needed her to realize that trying to scare someone was never a good thing. Didn't she learn anything from this case?

"I'll be sure to properly apologize to Aisha so she does not hold a grudge against you. That was the opposite effect that I desired."

"Thanks, Shelby." I could only shake my head. Leave it

to Shelby Holmes to use science and psychology to try to help me with Aisha, even though I was doing fine on my own.

Not that I—

Never mind.

"I think I have something that will make you feel better." Shelby pulled up a photo on her phone. It showed an angry Moira seated in an office between two adults who looked like they could be her parents. It was shot from a distance so you could see they were in a police station. "Lestrade sent it to me."

You know what, that did make me feel better.

"So, I have deduced that you are free for the rest of the afternoon," Shelby stated.

"Yeah, Shelby. Clearly I'm—"

But I stopped myself. Because it could only mean one thing.

I couldn't wait to hear her say it.

"We've got another case to solve."

ACKNOWLEDGMENTS

It's all treat and no trick getting to work on another Shelby and Watson book. Thank you so much to the incredible team at Bloomsbury for all their work on this series: Diane Aronson, Erica Barmash, Anna Bernard, Frank Bumbalo, Liz Byer, Danielle Ceccolini, Phoebe Dyer, Beth Eller, Courtney Griffin, Melissa Kavonic, Jeanette Levy, Cindy Loh, Donna Mark, Patricia McHugh, Linda Minton, Brittany Mitchell, Valentina Rice, Sarah Shumway, and Lily Yengle. Special thanks to my editor, Hali Baumstein, for making these books stronger and having to endure a special trip to eat ginormous ice cream sundaes.

Erwin Madrid deserves many bags of full-sized candy bars for his illustrations that bring Shelby and Watson to life.

Believe it or not (because I often don't), this is my twelfth published book. I'm so honored to get to write and never take it for granted. So much love to my family, friends, readers, and the wonderful booksellers, teachers, and librarians who have recommended my books. I couldn't do this without you. THANK YOU!